The Facetious Nights of Straparola, Volume 2 - Primary Source Edition

Giovanni Francesco Straparola, William George Waters, Girolamo Morlini

The
Italian Novelists

Volume Two

THE

ITALIAN
NOVELISTS

NOW FIRST TRANSLATED INTO
ENGLISH BY

W. G. WATERS

CHOICELY ILLUSTRATED BY

E. R. HUGHES, A.R.W.S., LONDON

In Seven Volumes
Volume II.

LONDON: PRIVATELY PRINTED
FOR MEMBERS OF THE SOCIETY
OF BIBLIOPHILES: MDCCCCI

The Incantation Of Cechato
Rabboso By Thia

———

Night the Fifth

FOURTH FABLE

The Incantation Of Cechato Rabboso By Thia

—

Night the Fifth

FOURTH FABLE

The Incantation Of Cechato Rabboso By Thia

Night the Fifth

FOURTH FABLE

THE

Facetious Nights

OF

STRAPAROLA

NOW FIRST TRANSLATED INTO
ENGLISH BY

W. G. WATERS

CHOICELY ILLUSTRATED BY

JULES GARNIER
AND E. R. HUGHES, A.R.W.S.

IN FOUR VOLUMES
VOLUME II.

LONDON: PRIVATELY PRINTED
FOR MEMBERS OF THE SOCIETY
OF BIBLIOPHILES: MDCCCCI ∴

THE FACETIOUS NIGHTS OF GIOVANNI FRANCESCO STRAPAROLA * * * * * * *

CONSISTS OF AN EXQUISITE AND DE-
LIGHTFUL COLLECTION OF HUMOROUS
WITTY AND MIRTHFUL CONVERSATIONS
FABLES AND ENIGMAS INCLUDING SING-
ING MUSIC AND DANCING • • • • • • •

DURING THE THIRTEEN NIGHTS
OF THE CARNIVAL AT VENICE

AS RELATED BY TEN CHARMING AND ACCOM-
PLISHED DAMSELS AND SEVERAL NOBLES
MEN OF LEARNING ILLUSTRIOUS AND HON-
ORABLE GENTLEMEN OF NOTE AT THE
ENTERTAINMENTS OF MERRIMENT AND
PLEASURE • • • • • • • • • • • • • • •

GIVEN BY THE PRINCESS LUCRETIA
AT HER BEAUTIFUL PALACE AT
MURANO • • • • • • • • • • • • • • •

Night the Fourth.

LREADY the golden-haired Apollo in his radiant chariot had sped away from this hemisphere of ours, and, having sunk beyond the distant line of sea, had betaken himself to the antipodes, and all those who had been labouring in the fields, now weary with their hard toil, felt no desire for aught save to repose quietly in their beds, when the worshipful and highborn company assembled themselves joyfully once more in the accustomed spot. And after the ladies and gentlemen had spent a short time in mirthful converse, the Signora Lucretia, when silence had been restored, bade them bring forth the golden vase. Then having written with her own hand the names of five of the ladies and cast them

3

into the vase, she called to the Signor
Vangelista and directed him to draw out
of the vase the names one by one, in
order that they might clearly know to
which of their companions the duty of
story-telling on that same night would be
assigned.   Then Signor Vangelista, rising from his seat, and breaking off the
pleasant discourse he was holding with
Lodovica, went obediently towards the
Signora, and, having sunk down upon
his knees reverently at her feet, he put
his hand in the vase, and drew out first
the name Fiordiana, then that of Vicenza,
then that of Lodovica, next that of Isabella, and last the name of Lionora.
But before they made a beginning of
their story-telling the Signora gave the
word to Molino and to the Trevisan that
they should take their lutes and sing a
ballad.   The two gentlemen did not wait
for any further command, but forthwith
tuned their instruments and sang to a
joyous strain the following verse:

SONG.

There is a face which is my sun of love,
   In whose kind warmth I breathe and move,
   Or faint beneath its scorching ray ;
And when it shines amongst the fairest fair,
   My lady reigns beyond compare,
And all around her bend beneath her sway.

Happy, thrice happy, is that favoured one,
   Who sees no face but hers alone,
   And passion's nectar eager sips,
Who listens to the music of her tongue,
   More sweet than lay by seraphs sung,
In words that fall like jewels from her lips.

But happier still were I if she benign
   Would place her lily hand in mine,
And mark me worthy such a prize to claim.
   Dull clod of earth although I be,
   Then should I full fruition see
Of every hope and end of every aim.

The song was attentively listened to
and warmly commended by every one of
the company. And when the Signora
saw that it had come to an end she directed Fiordiana, to whom had been as-

signed the first turn of story-telling on
this the fourth night, that she should
begin hers straightway, and follow the
order which had been observed since the
beginning of their entertainment; and
the damsel, who was no less eager to
speak than the rest of the company were
to listen, thus began her fable.

THE FIRST FABLE.

Ricardo, King of Thebes, had four daughters,
one of whom, having become a wanderer and
altered her name of Costanza to Costanzo,
arrived at the court of Cacco, King of Bettinia, who took her to wife on account of the
many worthy deeds wrought by her.

I MUST tell you, fair and gracious ladies, that the fable which
Eritrea told to us on the evening last past has brought me
into so bashful a mood that I feel but
little in the humour to act the story-
teller to-night. Nevertheless, the sense
of obedience I have for every command
of the Signora, and the respect I feel for

the whole of this honourable and gracious company, compels and encourages me to make trial with a certain story which, though it assuredly will not be found as pleasing as the one recently related by Eritrea, I will give you for what it is worth. You shall hear how a certain damsel, endowed with a noble soul and high courage, one who in the course of her noteworthy adventures was far better served by fortune than by reason, held it preferable to become a servant than to fall into a base manner of life; how, after enduring servitude for some time, she became the wife of King Cacco, and lived content with her reward. All this will be set forth to you in the story I am about to tell you.

In Egypt is situated the great and splendid city of Thebes, a place richly ornamented with noble buildings, public as well as private, situated in a country rich in cornfields growing white for the sickle, and favoured with fresh water in abundance; abounding, moreover, in all

those things which go to make up a glorious city.   In times long past this city
was under the rule of a king called by
name Ricardo, a man profoundly wise,
of great knowledge, and of the highest
valour.   Now this monarch, desiring
greatly to have an heir to his kingdom,
took to wife Valeriana, the daughter of
Marliano, King of Scotland, a lady who
was, in truth, perfection itself, very fair
to look upon, and exceedingly gracious.
Of her he begot three daughters, who
were gentle in their manners, full of
grace, and fair as rosebuds in the morning.   Of these one was called Valentia,
another Dorothea, and the third Spinella.
In the course of time it became manifest
to Ricardo that Valeriana his wife had
come to that season of life when women
commonly cease from child-bearing, and
that his three daughters were all of them
ripe for marriage, wherefore he determined forthwith to dispose of the three
princesses in honourable wedlock, and at
the same time to divide his kingdom into

three parts, whereof he proposed to give
one to each of his daughters, only keeping for himself so much as he judged
would suffice for the entertainment of
himself, and of his family, and of his
court. And all these plans he carried
out as he had deliberated with himself,
so that the result of his project proved
to be exactly what he had wished it to
be.

In due time the three maidens were
given in marriage to three powerful kings,
one to the King of Scardona, another to
the King of the Goths, and the third to
the King of Scythia ; and to each one
of them was assigned, by way of dowry,
a third part of their father's kingdom,
Ricardo himself keeping back only a
very small portion thereof to serve to
satisfy his vital needs. And thus the
good king, with Valeriana, his well-beloved wife, lived righteously in peace
and comfort. But it happened, after a
few years had passed, that the queen, of
whom the king expected no further off-

spring, proved to be with child, and at
the end of her time was brought to bed
with a very beautiful little girl, whom
the king welcomed with affection and
caresses as warm as he had given to the
other three children. But the queen
was not so well pleased with this last
infant, not, however, on account of any
dislike for the child herself, but because,
seeing that the kingdom was now divided
into three parts and given away, she
feared that there would be no chance of
furnishing this daughter with a dowry
sufficient to win her a marriage worthy
of their state. She desired at the same
time that the child should receive the
share due to a daughter of hers. But,
having handed over the child to the care
of a very competent nurse, she gave strict
command to her to use the greatest care
in her charge, to give the child good in-
struction, and to train her in the gentle
and praiseworthy manners and carriage
which become a fair and graceful maiden.
The child, to whom the name of Co-

stanza was given, grew day by day more
lovely and her manners more engaging,
nor could any subject from the most
learned masters be brought forward which
she would not at once apprehend most
readily. By the time Costanza was
twelve years of age she had already
learned to embroider, to sing, to dance,
to play the lute, and to do every one of
those feats which are rightly held to mark
a princess of rank. But, not content
with these graces, she gave herself also
to the study of polite letters, which
proved to be to her so great a source
of pleasure and delight that she would
spend over them not merely the day,
but the night as well, striving always to
find out the exquisite beauties of the
books she studied. And over and above
all these excellencies she mastered completely the art of war in learning how to
gentle horses, and to handle arms, and
to run in the lists as if she had been a
strong and well-trained man-at-arms and
not a damsel. In jousting, indeed, she

was so skilled that she ofttimes came out
of the contest victorious, just as if she
had been one of those valorous knights
who are held worthy of the highest
honour.   Wherefore, on account of all
these virtues, and on her own account
as well, Costanza was greatly loved by
the king and the queen and by all those
around them, so that there seemed to
be no limit to their affection.

When Costanza had come to a mar-
riageable age, the king her father, finding that he had now neither the state
nor the gold required to secure for her a
match with some potent sovereign equal
to her merits, was greatly troubled thereanent, and often took counsel with the
queen concerning the matter ; but the
prudent Valeriana, in whose sight the good
qualities of their child appeared to be so
many and so great that no other lady in
the land could in any way be put on a
level with her, was not disquieted at all,
and consoled the king with gentle and
loving words, bidding him keep a light

heart, and not to doubt at all but that in the end some powerful sovereign, fired with love by the many virtues of their daughter, would not disdain to take her to wife, even though they might not be able to give her a dowry.

Before many months had passed the damsel was sought in marriage by divers gallant gentlemen, amongst whom was Brunello, the son of the Marquis of Vivien, whereupon the king and the queen called their daughter to them into their chamber, and when they were all seated, the king spake thus: ' Costanza, my well-beloved child, the time is now come when it is meet that you should be married, and we have found for you as a husband a youth who ought to please your taste.   He is no other than the son of the Marquis of Vivien, our good friend and neighbour; his name is Brunello, and he is a graceful seemly youth, the report of his valorous deeds having spread already throughout the world.   And moreover he asks of us nought besides our own goodwill and your fair sweet self, upon which I put a value exceeding that of all the pomp and treasure of the world.   You must know that, though you are the daughter of a king, yet I cannot, on account of my poverty, find for you a more exalted alliance.   Wherefore you must be content with this establishment and conform to our wishes.'   The damsel, who was very prudent and conscious that she was sprung from high lineage, listened attentively to her father's words, and, without wasting any time over the matter, answered him as follows : ' Sacred majesty, there is no need that I should spend many words in replying to your honourable proposal, but simply that I should speak as the question between us demands.   And first I desire to testify to you my gratitude, the warmest I can express, for all the affection and benevolence you exhibit towards me in seeking to provide me with a husband without any request from me.   Next — speak-

ing with all submission and reverence —
I do not purpose to let myself fall below the race of my ancestors, who from
all time have been famous and illustrious, nor do I wish to debase the crown
you wear by taking for a husband one
who is our inferior. You, my beloved
father, have begotten four daughters, of
whom you have married three in the
most honourable fashion to three mighty
kings, giving with them great store of
gold and wide domains, but you wish to
dispose of me, who have ever been obedient to you and observant of your pre-
cepts, in an ignoble alliance. Wherefore
I tell you, to end my speech, that I will
never take a husband unless I can be
mated, like my three sisters, to a king of
a rank that is my due.' Shortly after
this, Costanza, shedding many tears the
while, took leave of the king and queen,
and, having mounted a gallant horse, set
forth from Thebes alone, and determined
to follow whatever road fortune might
lay open to her feet.

While she was thus journeying at hazard she deemed it wise to change her name, so in lieu of Costanza she called herself Costanzo, and donned a man's attire. She passed over many mountain ranges, and lakes, and marshes, and saw many lands, and heard the tongues and took heed of the ways and manners of certain races who live their lives after the fashion of brutes rather than of men. At last, one day at the set of sun, she arrived at a famed and celebrated city called Costanza, the capital of all the country round, and at that time under the rule of Cacco, King of Bettinia. And, having entered therein, she forthwith began to admire the superb palaces, the straight roomy streets, the running water, the broad rivers, and the clear, soft, trickling fountains. Then, when she had come near to the piazza, she saw the spacious and lofty palace of the king, adorned with columns of the finest marble and porphyry, and, having raised her eyes somewhat, she saw the king,

who was standing upon a gallery which
commanded a view of the whole piazza,
and taking off her cap from her head
she made him a profound reverence.
The king, when he perceived the fair
and graceful youth down below, had him
called and brought into his presence,
and as soon as Costanzo stood before
him he demanded from what country he
had come, and by what name he was
called. The youth, with a smiling face,
gave answer that he had journeyed from
Thebes, driven thence by envious and
deceitful fortune, and that Costanzo was
his name. He declared, moreover, that
he desired greatly to attach himself to
the service of some gentleman of worth,
pledging himself to serve any such lord
with all the faith and affection that good
service merited. The king, who meantime was mightily pleased with the appearance of the youth, said to him:
‘ Seeing that you bear the name of this
my city, it is my pleasure that you tarry
here in my court with no other duty

laid upon you than to attend to my person.'   The youth, who desired no better office than this, first rendered to the king his gratitude, and then joyfully accepted service under him as lord, offering at the same time to hold himself ready to discharge any duty which might be assigned to him.

So Costanza, in the guise of a man, entered into the service of the king, and served him so well and gracefully that every one who came near him was astonished beyond measure at his talents. And it chanced that the queen, when she had well observed and considered the graceful bearing, the pleasant manners, and the discreet behaviour of Costanzo, began to cast her eyes more diligently upon him, until at last, so hotly did she grow inflamed with love of him, neither by day nor by night did she turn her thoughts upon any other.   And so soft and so loving were the glances that she would continually dart towards him, that not only a youth, but even the hardest rock, or the unyielding diamond even, might well have been softened. Wherefore the queen, being thus consumed with passion for Costanzo, yearned for nothing else than that she might some day find occasion to foregather with him alone. And before long it came to pass that chance gave her the opportunity of conversing with him, so she straightway inquired of him whether it would be agreeable to him to enter into her service, making it known to him likewise that by serving her he would gain, over and above the guerdon which she would give him, the approbation or even the reverence and respect of all the court.

Costanzo perceived clearly enough that these words which came out of the queen's mouth sprang from no goodwill of hers for his advancement, but from amorous passion. Knowing moreover, that, being a woman like herself, he could in no way satisfy the hot unbridled lust which prompted them, with unclouded face he humbly made answer to her in these words : ' Signora, so strong is the obligation of service which binds me to my lord your husband, that it seems to me I should be working him a base injury were I to withdraw myself from my obedience to his will. Therefore I pray you to hold me excused, and to pardon me that I am not ready and willing at once to take service with you, and to accept, as the reason of this my refusal of your gracious offer, my resolve to serve my lord even unto death, provided that it pleases him to retain me as his man.' And, having taken leave of the queen, he withdrew from her presence. The queen, who was well aware that men do not fell to earth a hard oak-tree with a single stroke, many and many a time after this made trial, with the deepest cunning and art, to entice the youth to take service under her, but he, as constant and as strong as a lofty tower beaten by the winds, was not to be moved. As soon as the queen became conscious of this, the ardent burning love

in her was turned to mortal bitter hatred,
so that she could no longer bear the sight
of him. And, having now grown anxious to work his destruction, she pondered day and night how she might best
set to work to clear him out of her path,
but she was in great dread of the king,
for that he continued to hold the youth
in high favour.

In a certain district of the province of
Bettinia there was to be found a strange
race of beings, in whom one-half of the
body, that is to say, the upper part, was
made after the fashion of a man, though
they had ears like those of animals, and
horns as well. But in their lower parts
they had members resembling those of
a rough shaggy goat, with a little tail,
twisted and curling, of the sort one sees
upon a pig. These creatures were called
satyrs, and by their depredations they
caused great loss and damage to the villages and the farms and the people living
in the country thereabout. Wherefore
the king desired greatly to have one of

these satyrs taken alive and delivered
over into his keeping, but there was
found no one about the court with heart
stout enough to undertake this adventure and capture a satyr for the king.
By sending him on an errand of this sort
the queen hoped to work Costanzo's destruction, but the issue of the matter was
not at all what she desired, for in this
case, as in many others, the would-be de-
ceiver, by the workings of divine provi-
dence and supreme justice, was cast
under the feet of the one she purposed
to beguile.

The treacherous queen, being well
aware of the king's longing, happened
to be one day in converse with him concerning divers matters, and, while they
were thus debating, she said to him :
' My lord, have you never considered
that Costanzo, your faithful and devoted
servant, is strong and vigorous enough
in body, and daring and courageous
enough in soul, to go and capture for
you one of these satyrs, and to bring him

back to you alive, without calling on
anyone else to aid him. If the matter
should fall out in this wise, as I believe
it would, you might easily make trial of
it, and in the course of an hour attain
the wish of your heart, and Costanzo,
as a brave and valiant knight, would enjoy the honour of the deed, which would
be accounted to him for glory for ever.'
This speech of the cunning queen pleased
the king greatly, and he straightway bade
them summon Costanzo into his presence.
When the youth appeared the king thus
addressed him : ' Costanzo, if indeed you
love me, as you make show of doing,
and as all people believe, you will now
carry out fully the wish I have in my
heart, and you yourself shall possess the
glory of the fulfilling thereof. You are
surely aware that what I desire more
than aught else in the world is to have
a satyr alive in my own keeping. Wherefore, seeing how strong and active you
are, I reckon there is no other man in
all my kingdom so well fitted to work

my will in this affair as you ; so, loving
me as you do, you will not refuse to
carry out my will.' The youth, who
suspected not that this demand sprang
from aught else than the king's desire,
was anxious to give no cause of vexation
to the king, and with a cheerful and amiable face thus made answer : ' My lord,
in this and in everything else you may
command me. However weak and imperfect my faculties may be, I will on
no account draw back from striving to
fulfil your wishes, even though in the
task I should meet with my death. But,
before I commit myself to this perilous
adventure, I beg you, my lord, that you
will cause to be taken into the wood
where the satyrs abide a large vessel with
a wide mouth of the same size as those
which the servants use in dressing smooth
the shifts and other kinds of body linen.
And besides this I would have taken
thither a large cask of good white wine,
the best that can be had and the strongest, together with two bags full of the

finest white bread.' The king forthwith
bade them get in readiness everything
which Costanzo had described, and Costanzo then journeyed towards the wood
in question. Having arrived there he
took a copper bucket and began to fill
it with white wine drawn from the cask,
and this he poured into the other vessel
which stood near by. Next he took
some of the bread, and, having broken
it in pieces, he put these into the vessel
full of wine. This being done he climbed
up into a thick-leaved tree which stood
hard by, and waited to see what might
happen next.

Costanzo had not been long up in the
tree before the satyrs, who had smelt
the odour of the fragrant wine, began to
draw near to the vessel, and having come
close to it, each one swilled therefrom a
good bellyfull of wine, greedy as the hungry wolves when they fall upon a fold of
young lambs. And after they had filled
their stomachs and had taken enough,
they lay down to sleep, and so sound and

deep was their slumber that all the noise
in the world would not have roused them.
Then Costanzo, seeing that the time
for action had come, descended from the
tree and went softly up to one of the
satyrs, whose hands and feet he bound
fast with a cord he had brought with him.
Next, without making any noise, he laid
him upon his horse and carried him off.
And while Costanzo was on his way back,
with the satyr tightly bound behind him,
they came at the vesper hour to a village
not far from the city, and the creature,
who by this time had recovered from the
effects of the wine, woke up and began
to yawn as if he were rising from his bed.
Looking around him he perceived the
father of a family, who with a crowd
around him was going to bury a dead
child, weeping bitterly the while, and the
priest, who conducted the service, was
singing. When he looked upon this
spectacle the satyr began to laugh mightily. Afterwards, when they had entered
the city and were come to the piazza, the

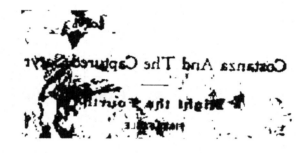

Costanza And The Captured Satyr

Night the Fourth

FIRST FABLE

Costanza And The Captured Satyr

—

Night the Fourth

FIRST FABLE

satyr beheld a great crowd of people who
were staring open-mouthed at a poor lad
who had just mounted the gallows to be
hanged by the executioner, and the satyr
laughed thereat even louder than he had
laughed before.   And afterwards, when
they were come to the palace, a great
joy seized upon the people standing by,
and they all cried out 'Costanzo! Costanzo!'   And the satyr, when he heard
this shouting, laughed louder than ever.

When Costanzo was conducted into
the presence of the king and of the queen
and her ladies, he presented to the king
the satyr, who thereupon laughed again,
and so loud and long was his laughter
that all those that were there present
were not a little astonished.   After this
the king, seeing with what diligence Costanzo had fulfilled his dearest wish, held
him in as high affection and esteem as
ever lord extended to servant, but this
humour of his only added fresh griefs to
the load which already lay upon the
queen's heart ; for that, having schemed

to ruin Costanzo, she had done nothing but exalt him to yet greater honour. Wherefore the wicked queen, not being able to endure the sight of such great prosperity as had come to Costanzo, devised yet another snare for him, which was this. She knew that the king was wont to go every morning to the cell where the satyr was kept in hold, and for his diversion would essay to make the creature talk, but as yet he had in no wise succeeded in his efforts. Wherefore, having sought out the king, she said to him: 'Sire, you have betaken yourself over and over again to the satyr's cell, and you have wearied yourself in your endeavours to induce him to talk with you in order that you might take diversion therefrom, but the creature still shows no sign of speaking a word. Why, therefore, should you further worry your brains over this affair, for you may take it for certain that, if Costanzo were only willing, he could easily make the satyr converse and answer questions.'

The king, when he listened to these words, straightway bade them summon Costanzo into his presence, and when he came the king thus addressed him: 'Costanzo, I am well assured that you know how great is the pleasure I get from the satyr you captured for me; nevertheless it irks me greatly to find that he is dumb, and will never make any answer to the words I say to him and the questions I put. If you would only do all that you might, I am sure that you would be able to make him speak.' 'Sire,' Costanzo replied, 'that the satyr is dumb is no fault of mine; it is not the office of a mortal, like me, to make him speak, but of a god. But if the reason of his muteness comes not from any natural or accidental defect, but from stubborn resolve to keep silence, I will do all that lies in my power to make him open his mouth in speech.' Then, having gone together to the satyr's prison, they gave him some dainty food, and some wine still better, and called out to him, 'Eat, Chiappino' (for this was the name they had given to the satyr). But the creature only stared at them without uttering a word. Then they went on: 'Come, Chiappino, tell us whether that capon and that wine are to your taste;' but still he was silent. Costanzo, perceiving how obstinate the humour of the creature was, said, 'So you will not answer me, Chiappino. Let me tell you you are doing a very foolish thing, seeing that I can if I will let you die of hunger here in prison.' And at these words the satyr shot a sideglance at Costanzo. After a little Costanzo went on: 'Answer me, Chiappino; for if you speak to me (as I hope you will) I will liberate you from this place.' Then Chiappino, who had listened with eagerness to all that had been said, answered, as soon as he heard speak of liberation, 'What will you of me?' Costanzo then said, 'Tell me, have you eaten and drunk well?' 'Yes,' said Chiappino. 'Now I want you, of your courtesy, to tell me,' said Costanzo, 'what

thing it was that moved you to laughter
in the village street when we met with the
body of the child on its way to be buried?'
To this Chiappino answered, 'I laughed,
indeed, not at the dead child, but at the
so-called father, to whom the child in
the coffin was in fact no kin at all, and I
laughed at the priest singing the office,
who was the real father,' by which speech
the satyr would have them understand
that the mother of the child had carried
on an intrigue with the priest.   Then
said Costanzo, 'And now I want to
know, my Chiappino, what it was that
made you laugh yet louder when we were
come into the piazza?'   'I laughed
then,' replied Chiappino, 'to see a thousand or more thieves, who had robbed the
public purse of crowns by the million,
who deserved a thousand gibbets, standing in the piazza to feast their eyes on
the sight of a poor wretch led to the gallows, who, perchance, had merely pilfered
ten florins wherewith to buy bread for
himself and his poor children.   That

was why I laughed.' Then said Costanzo, ' And besides this, I beg you to
tell me how it was that, when we were
come into the palace, you laughed longer
and louder than ever ? '   ' Ah, I beg you
will not trouble me more at present,'
said Chiappino, ' but go your way and
come back to-morrow, and then I will
answer you and tell you certain things
of which perchance you have no inkling.'
When Costanzo heard this, he said to
the king, ' Let us depart and come back
to-morrow, and hear what this thing may
be.'   Whereupon the king and Costanzo
took their leave, and gave orders that
Chiappino should be given to eat and
drink of the best, and that he should be
allowed to chatter as he would.

When the next day had come they
both went to see Chiappino, and they
found him puffing and blowing like a
great pig, and, having gone close to him,
cried out to him several times in a loud
voice.   But Chiappino, who had well
filled his belly, answered nought.   Then

Costanzo gave him a sharp prick with a dart which he had with him, whereupon the satyr awoke and stood up and demanded who was there. 'Now get up, Chiappino,' said Costanzo, 'and tell us that thing which yesterday you promised we should hear, and say why you laughed so loud when we came to the palace?' To which question Chiappino made this reply : 'For a reason which you ought to understand better than I. It was, forsooth, at hearing them all shouting, "Costanzo! Costanzo!" while all the time you are Costanza.' The king when he heard this could in no wise comprehend what this saying of Chiappino's might mean ; but Costanzo, who immediately recognized its import, in order to keep him from speaking more, at once stopped the way for him [1] by saying : 'And when you had been brought into the very presence of the king and queen, what made you laugh then as if nothing could stop you?' To this Chiappino

[1] Orig., *gli troncò la strada.*

made answer: 'I laughed then so out-
rageously because the king, and you as
well, believed that the maidens who were
in service on the queen were really
maidens, whereas the greater part of them
were young men.' And then he was
silent.

When the king heard these words he
knew not what to think, but he said
nothing; and, having left the wild satyr,
he went out with Costanzo, wishing to
learn clearly what might be the meaning
of what he had heard. And after he had
made · due inquiry he found that Costanzo was in truth a woman, and not a
youth, and that the supposed damsels
about the queen were sprightly young
men, as Chiappino had said. And
straightway the king bade them light a
great fire in the middle of the piazza,
and into it, in the presence of all the
people, he caused to be cast the queen
and all her paramours. And, bearing in
mind the praiseworthy loyalty and the
open faithfulness of Costanza, and mark-

ing moreover her exceeding beauty, the king made her his wife in the presence of all his barons and knights. When he knew who her parents were, he greatly rejoiced, and forthwith despatched ambassadors to King Ricardo and to Valeriana his wife, and to the three sisters of Costanza, to tell them how she was now the wife of a king; whereupon they all felt the joy due to such good news. Thus the noble Costanza, in recompense for the faithful service she rendered, became a queen and lived long with Cacco her husband.

When Fiordiana had brought her fable to an end, the Signora made a sign to her to give her enigma. The damsel, who was somewhat haughty, rather by chance than by nature, set it forth in the following words:

> Over savage lions twain
> A spirit soft and mild doth reign.
> By her side four damsels move,
> Prudence, Valour, Faith, and Love.
> She bears a sword in her right hand;
> Before it calm the righteous stand,

But wicked men and souls unjust
It smites and lays them in the dust.
Discord nor wrong with her may rest,
And he who loves her wins the best.

This clever enigma set forth by Fiordiana, who indeed was a damsel of subtle
mind, won the praise of all, and some
found its meaning to be one thing, and
some another. But there was no one of
all the company who rightly divined it,
seeing that all their solutions were far
wide of the true one. When Fiordiana
saw this she said in a lively tone, " Ladies
and gentlemen, I see you are troubling
yourselves in vain, seeing that my enigma means nothing else than that infinite
and equal justice which like a gentle
spirit rules and restrains both the hungry, savage lions, and likewise the proud,
unconquerable spirit of man. More
than that, justice makes steadfast her
faith, holding in her right hand a sharp
sword, and accompanied always by four
virgins, Prudence, Charity, Fortitude,
and Faith. She is gentle and kind to

the good, and severe and bitter to the
perverse and bad." When Fiordiana
ceased speaking, the listeners were greatly
pleased with the interpretation of her
enigma. Then the Signora bade the
gracious Vicenza to follow in her turn
with a fable, and she, eager to obey this
command, spake as follows.

THE SECOND FABLE.

Erminione Glaucio, an Athenian, takes to wife
Filenia Centurione, and, having become jealous
of her, accuses her before the tribunal, but by
the help of Hippolito, her lover, she is acquitted
and Erminione punished.

F a truth, gracious ladies, there
would be in all the world no
condition more sweet, more
delightful, or more happy than
the service of love, were it not for that
bitter fruit which springs from sudden
jealousy, the foe which drives away
gentle Cupid, the betrayer of kindly
ladies, the foe who day and night tries
to compass their death. Wherefore there

comes into my recollection a fable which ought to be received by you with some satisfaction, seeing that from it you will be able readily to understand the hard and piteous fate which befell a gentleman of Athens, who, because of his impotent jealousy, sought the taking off of his wife by the sword of justice, but was instead condemned himself, and met his death thereby. Which judgment ought to please you, because, if I am not greatly in error, you are yourselves all of you more or less in love.

In Athens, the most ancient city of Greece, and one which was in times past the veritable home and resort of all learning, though now, through her flighty vanity, entirely ruined and overthrown, there resided once upon a time a gentleman named Messer Erminione Glaucio, a man of much consideration and repute in the city, rich in purse, but at the same time of mean intelligence. Now it chanced that when he was an old man, finding himself without progeny, he made up his mind to marry, and he took to wife a damsel named Filenia, daughter of Messer Cesarino Centurione, of noble descent and gifted with marvellous beauty and with good qualities out of number. In short, there was in all the city no other maiden who was her equal. And, for-asmuch as he was greatly in fear lest his wife, on account of her marvellous beauty, should be courted by divers of the gal-lants of the city, and perhaps give occa-sion for some disgraceful scandal, through which the finger of scorn might be pointed at him, he resolved to restrain her in a certain lofty tower of his palace, out of sight of all passers-by. And before long it happened that the wretched old dotard, without knowing why, let his jealousy rise to such a pitch that he mistrusted even himself.

There was residing in the city at this time a certain scholar of Crete, young in years, but very discreet, and greatly loved and esteemed by all who knew him on account of his amiability and grace.

The name of this youth was Hippolito, and before Filenia was married he had paid suit to her, and, besides this, he was on intimate terms with Messer Erminione, who held him as dear as if he had been his own son. At a certain time during his scholar's course he found himself somewhat disinclined for study ; so, desiring to recruit his spirits, he took his departure from Athens, and having gone into Crete, he sojourned there for a time, to discover on his return that Filenia was married. On this account he fell into an access of melancholy, and he grieved the more because he was now deprived of all hope of seeing her at his pleasure, nor could he endure to remember that a maiden so lovely and graceful should be bound in marriage to a toothless, slobbering old man.

Wherefore the love-stricken Hippolito, finding himself no longer able to endure the burning pricks and the sharp arrows of love, set himself to find out some method, some hidden way by which

he might enjoy the fulfilment of his desires. And after he had well considered
the many schemes which presented themselves to him, he fixed at last upon a
certain one which appeared to him the
most fitting. To put this in execution
he first betook himself to the shop of a
carpenter, his neighbour, where he ordered to be made two chests of the same
length and breadth and width, and of the
same measure and quality, so that no one
would be able to distinguish the one from
the other. This done, he repaired to
Messer Erminione's house, and, making
pretense of wanting something of him,
spake in cunning wise the following
words: ' Messer Erminione, you know
well enough that I love and reverence you
as if you were my own father, and for my
part if I were not well convinced of your
affection for myself, I would never dare,
with such assurance as I now use, to beg
any favour of you ; but, seeing that I
have ever found you well disposed to
me, I am wellnigh certain that I shall

now get from you that service which
my heart so greatly desires. It happens
that I am constrained to leave Athens
and to go to the city of Frenna to expe-
dite some very important matters of
business, and I must remain there until
such time as these shall be completed.
And because I have no one about me
whom I can fully trust, seeing that I am
served only by menials and hirelings, of
whom I am in no way well assured, I
would fain that you hold in charge for
me — provided that it be your pleasure
so to do — a certain chest of mine full
of articles of value which I happen to
possess.' Messer Erminione, suspecting
nought of the craft of the young scholar,
made answer to him that he was well
content to grant this favour, and that for
greater security the chest should be de-
posited and kept in the same chamber
in which he slept. On hearing this reply the scholar returned to Messer Erminione his thanks, the warmest he
knew how to render, promising the while

to keep in mind the memory of this
. great favour done to him as long as he
should live. Then he begged the old
man to do him the honour to go with him
as far as his own dwelling, in order that
he might exhibit to him the various articles which he had stored in the chest.
Wherefore the two, having gone together
to the house of Hippolito, the latter
pointed out a chest filled with rich garments and jewels and necklaces of no
small value, and then, having summoned
a certain one of his servants and presented him to Messer Erminione, he
said: 'If at any time, Messer Erminione,
this my servant should be seeing after
the removal of my chest, you can trust
him to the full as if he were my own
self.' And when Messer Erminione
had taken his departure Hippolito hid
himself in the other chest, which was
exactly like the one filled with garments
and jewels, and having fastened it from
the inside, he bade his servant carry it to
a certain place he knew of. The servant,

who was privy to the affair, obedient to his master's order called a porter, and having lifted the burden on the man's back, ordered him to bear it to the tower in which was situated the chamber where Messer Erminione slept every night with his young wife.

Messer Erminione, being one of the chiefs of the city and a man of wealth and influence, it fell to his lot, on account of the worshipful state he filled, to go for a certain space of time to a place called Porto Pireo, distant about twenty stadi from the city of Athens, and there to compose certain suits and strifes which had arisen between the townsmen and the peasants round about — albeit he found this errand but little to his taste. Wherefore, when Messer Erminione had gone his way, tormented as ever by the jealousy which day and night weighed upon him, the youth, shut up in the chest which now stood in Madonna Filenia's bedroom, was waiting for the favourable moment. More than once had

he heard the fair dame weeping and sigh-
ing as she bemoaned her hard lot, and
the place and the hour which had seen
her given in marriage to a miserable old
man who had proved to be the ruin of
her life. And when it seemed to him
that she was in her first sleep, he got
out of the chest, and, having gone to the
bedside, said in a soft voice: 'Awake,
my soul! for I, your Hippolito, am
here.' And when she was fully aroused,
and saw him and knew who he was (for
there was a candle burning in the chamber), she was inclined to cry out; but
the young man, putting his hand upon
her lips, would not allow this, and thus
addressed her in a voice full of agita-
tion: 'Be silent, heart of mine! do you
not see that I am Hippolito, your faithful lover? Of a truth I cannot live
apart from you.' The fair young woman
was somewhat comforted by these words,
and by the time she had found the opportunity for comparing the worth of her
old husband with the youthful Hippo-

lito, she was by no means ill-satisfied
with the turn things had taken, and lay
all night with her lover, spending the
time in loving conversation and railing
at the impotent ways of her doltish husband. Before they parted they agreed
together to meet again in like manner,
and when the morning began to dawn
the youth got back into his chest, and
every evening would issue therefrom and
spend the night with the lady.

Now, after a good many days had
elapsed, Messer Erminione, giving the
business good speed both on account of
the discomfort he himself suffered and
of the rabid jealousy which never ceased
to torment him, put an end to all the dis-
putes he had been called upon to settle,
and went back to his home. The servant of Hippolito, as soon as he heard
the news of Messer Erminione's return,
went without losing time to his house,
and, according to the agreement which
had been settled, demanded of him in
the name of his master Hippolito the

return of the chest, and this Messer Erminione gave up to him without a word
of demur. Wherefore, having summoned a porter, the servant caused the
chest to be conveyed home. Then Hippolito, having come out of his hiding-
place, went forthwith to the piazza, where
he met with Messer Erminione, and after
he had embraced him, he thanked him
most courteously in the warmest terms
he could find for the great kindness he
had received, and at the same time declared that he himself and all that he
possessed should ever be ready at Messer Erminione's service.

It chanced that on a certain morning
Messer Erminione remained in bed with
his wife somewhat later than was his
wont, and, lifting up his eyes, he remarked upon the wall and high above
his head certain stains which looked as
if they had been caused by someone
spitting thereon. Wherefore his inveter-
ate jealousy began once more to trouble
him, and he was mightily amazed at

what he saw, and began to turn it over
in his mind in such wise that, after he
had well considered the matter, he could
not bring himself to believe that the
marks on the wall in question were any
work of his.   Then, with strong appre-
hension as to their meaning, he turned
to his wife and with an angry troubled
face demanded of her: ' What have you
to say about those spit marks high up
on the wall there?   I am well assured
they were never made by me, for I never
spat up there in my life.   I strongly sus-
pect that you have betrayed my honour.'
Filenia, laughing the while at this speech,
thus answered him: ' Is there no other
charge you would like to bring against
me?'   Messer Erminione, when he saw
her begin to laugh, grew more infuriated
than ever, and said: 'Ah, you laugh, do
you, wicked woman that you are?   Now,
tell me quickly what it is that makes
you laugh.'   'I am laughing,' answered
Filenia, 'at your own foolishness.'   At
these words Messer Erminione began to

chafe with rage,[1] and, being anxious to
make trial of his own powers and to see
whether he could spit so high, with
much coughing and gasping he strained
with all his might to reach the mark on
the wall by his spitting, but he wearied
himself in vain, for the spittle always
fell down again and lighted upon his
visage, plastering him thickly with filth.
And after the wretched old man had
made this trial many times, he found
that he only got in worse case every
turn. So, by the light of this experience, he persuaded himself that his wife
had assuredly played him false, and,
turning to her, he began to assail her
with the most rascally words that could
be applied to a guilty woman, and, if he
had not been in fear of the law and of
his own neck, he would surely have slain
her then and there with his own hands,
but he managed to restrain himself, deeming it better to deal with her by legal
process than to stain his hands in her

---

[1] Orig., *tra se stesso se radeva.*

blood.   Not satisfied with the rating he had already given her, he betook himself, full of wrath and anger, to the tribunal, where he preferred before the judge a charge of adultery against h¹s wife.   But, seeing that it lay not within the power of the judge to pronounce condemnation upon her unless the legal statutes should have been duly observed, he ordered Filenia to be brought before him in order that he might narrowly examine her.

Now, there was in Athens a law, which was held in the highest reverence, providing that any woman who might be charged by her husband with adultery should be placed at the foot of a certain red column, round which was entwined a serpent, and there make oath whether or not the accusation of adultery brought against her were true.   And after she had taken the oath she was required forthwith to put her hand in the serpent's mouth, and then, if she should have sworn falsely, the serpent would at once bite off her hand; otherwise, she received no injury. Hippolito, who had already heard rumours of this charge before the tribunal, and that the judge had sent to fetch Filenia to put her on her defence, being a youth of resource at once took action to see that she should not run into the snares of ignominious death. By way of rescuing her from condemnation he first of all stripped off all his clothes and donned in their stead some rags befitting a madman, and then, without being seen by anyone, he left his own lodging and ran straight to the tribunal as if he had been some one out of his mind, acting well the part of a crazy man as he went along the streets.

Now it chanced that while the officers of the court were haling along the poor lady towards the tribunal, all the people of the city gathered themselves together to take note as to how the cause would end, and in the midst of the crowd the pretended madman, forcing his way now here, now there, worked himself so well

Hippolito's Strategy To Save Filenia

Night the Fourth

SECOND FABLE

to the front that he found opportunity
to cast his arms round the neck of the
woeful lady, and to press a kiss upon her
lips, which caress she, seeing that her
arms were bound behind her back, could
in no wise escape. When the young
woman had been brought into the presence of the tribunal the judge addressed
her in these words : ' As you may see,
Filenia, your husband Messer Erminione is here to lay complaint against you
that you have committed adultery, and
furthermore prays that I should deal out
to you the due penalty according to the
statute ; wherefore you must now make
oath and say whether or not the charge
which your husband brings against you
is true.' Then the young woman, who
was very wary and keen of intellect,
swore with confidence that no man had
ever touched her save her husband and
the madman who was now present before them all. Then, after she had sworn,
the underlings of the court led her to
the place where was the serpent, which,

Hippolito's Strategy To Save Filenia

Night the Fourth

SECOND FABLE

Hippolito's Strategy To Save Filenia

Night the Fourth

SECOND FABLE

Hippolito's Strategy To Save Filenia

Night the Fourth

SECOND FABLE

after Filenia's hand had been placed in its mouth, did her no harm whatever, inasmuch as what she had sworn was really the truth, namely, that no man had ever given her caress of any sort except her husband and the so-called madman.

When they perceived this, the crowd, and all her kinsfolk, who had come thither to see the solemn and terrible sight, at once set her down as innocent and wrongfully accused, and cried out that Messer Erminione deserved the same death which was the penalty of the crime imputed to his wife. But, for the reason that he was a noble, a man of high lineage, and one of the chiefs of the city, the president would not permit him to be publicly burned (for so much power the law gave him), but, in order that he might duly discharge his office, he sentenced Erminione to be thrown into prison, where, after a short space of time, he expired. This is the wretched end which Messer Erminione put to his

senseless jealousy, and by these means
the young wife was delivered from an
ignominious death.   Before great length
of time had passed Hippolito made her
his lawful wife, and they lived many
years happily together.

When the story told by the discreet
and modest Vicenza had come to an end
— a story which pleased all the ladies
mightily — the Signora bade her to propound her enigma in due course, and
she, raising her pretty smiling face, instead of one of her songs gave the
following riddle:

> When hope and love and strong desire
> Are born to set the world on fire,
> That self-same hour a beast is born,
> All savage, meagre, and forlorn.
> Sometimes, with seeming soft and kind,
> Like ivy round an elm-tree twined,
> It clips us close with bine and leaf,
> But feeds on heartache, woe, and grief.
> Ever in mourning garb it goes,
> In anguish lives, in sorrow grows.
> And worse than worst the fate of him
> Who falls beneath its talons grim.

Here Vicenza brought her enigma to
an end. The interpretations of its meaning were diverse, and no one of the
company was found clever enough to
fathom its true import. When Vicenza
saw this, she sighed a little impatiently,
and then, with a smiling face, spake as
follows: " The enigma I have set you
to guess means nothing else than chil-
ling jealousy, which, all lean and faded,
is born at the same birth with love itself,
and winds itself round men and women
as well, just as the gently-creeping ivy
embraces the trunk so dear to it. This
jealousy feeds on heartache, seeing that
a jealous one always lives in anguish and
moves about in sombre garb on account
of the continual melancholy that torments him." This explication of the
enigma gave great pleasure to all, and
especially to Signora Chiara, whose husband had a temper somewhat jealous.
But, to let no one say to himself that
Vicenza's enigma had been framed to fit
his case, the Signora bade them at once

put a stop to their laughter, and signed
to Lodovica, whose turn it was to tell
the next story, that she should forthwith
begin, and the damsel opened her fable
in the following words.

THE THIRD FABLE.

Ancilotto, King of Provino, takes to wife the
daughter of a baker, and has by her three
children. These, after much persecution at
the hands of the king's mother, are made known
to their father through the strange working of
certain water, and of an apple, and of a bird.

HAVE always understood,
lovesome and gracious ladies,
that man is the noblest and
most capable of the living
creatures fashioned by nature, seeing that
God made him in His own image and
similitude, and willed that he should rule
and not be ruled.   And on this account
it is said that man is the perfect animal,
and of greater excellence than any of the
others, because all these, not even ex-
cepting woman, are subject to him.

Therefore, those who by deceit and cunning compass the death of so noble a creature commit a foul crime. And there is no wonder if sometimes those who work for the bane of others run heedlessly into destruction themselves, as did four women I have to tell of, who, in trying to destroy others, were themselves cut off and made a wretched end. All this you will readily understand from the fable I purpose to tell you.

In Provino, a very famous and royal city, there lived in ancient times three sisters, fair of person, gracious in manners, and courteous in bearing, but of base lineage, being the daughters of a certain Messer Rigo, a baker who baked bread for other folk in his oven. Of these one was named Brunora, another Lionella, and another Chiaretta. It happened one day when the three sisters were in their garden, and there taking much delight, that Ancilotto the king, who was going to enjoy the diversion of hunting with a great company, passed

that way. Brunora, the eldest sister,
when she looked upon the fair and noble assemblage, said to her sisters Lionella and Chiaretta, 'If I had for my
husband the king's majordomo, I flatter
myself that I would quench the thirst of
all the court with one glass of wine.'
'And I,' said Lionella, 'flatter myself
that, if the king's private chamberlain
were my husband, I would pledge myself to make enough linen from a spin-
dle of my yarn to provide shifts of the
strongest and finest make for all the
court.' Then said Chiaretta, 'And I, if
I had the king himself for my husband,
I flatter myself that I would give him
three children at one birth, two sons and
a daughter. And each of these should
have long hair braided below the shoulders, and intermingled with threads of
the finest gold, and a golden necklace
round the throat, and a star on the forehead of each.'

Now it chanced that these sayings
were overheard by one of the courtiers,

who hastened to the king and told him
of the young girls' discourse, and the
king, when he heard the tenour thereof,
at once commanded that they should be
brought before him, and this done, he
examined them one by one as to what
they had said in the garden. Whereupon each one, with the most respectful
words, told the king what she had
spoken, and he was much pleased thereat.
So then and there he wedded Brunora
to the majordomo and Lionella to the
chamberlain, while he himself took Chiaretta to wife. There was no hunting
that day, for the whole company returned
to the city, where the marriages were celebrated with the greatest pomp. But the
mother of Ancilotto was greatly wroth
at his marriage, for however fair Chiaretta might be in face and figure, and
graceful in her person, and sweet and
modest in her conversation, the queen-
mother held it to be a slight to the royal
dignity that her daughter-in-law should
be of vile and common descent, nor could

she endure it that the majordomo and
the chamberlain should be brothers-in-
law of the king her son. These things
kindled so hotly the rage of the queen-
mother against Chiaretta that she could
scarce endure her presence; nevertheless
she hid her wrath so as not to offend her
son. In due time (by the good pleasure
of Him who rules over all), Chiaretta became with child, to the great joy of the
king, whose fancy at once busied itself
with the prospect of the lovely progeny
he had been promised.

Just at the time when Chiaretta was
expecting to be brought to bed, Ancilotto
was forced to make a journey to a distant country and to abide there some
days, and he directed that, during his absence, his mother should see to the welfare of the queen and of the children
who, he hoped, would soon be born.
The queen-mother, though she hated
her daughter-in-law, let not the king see
this, and assured him that she would take
the greatest care of them all, while he

might be away, and before the king had
been gone many days (as Chiaretta when
she was a virgin had pledged) three
lovely children, two boys and a girl,
were born. Likewise their hair was
braided below their shoulders, and they
bore golden chains on their necks and
golden stars on their foreheads. The
queen-mother, whose hatred against Chiaretta burned as malignantly as ever, no
sooner cast her eyes upon the innocent
children than she determined to have
them put away privily, so that no one
might know they had even been, and
that Chiaretta might be disgraced in the
sight of the king. And besides this,
Brunora and Lionella had grown to regard their sister with violent hate and
jealousy since she had become their sovereign, and lost no chance to aggravate,
by all sorts of cunning wiles, the spite
of the queen-mother against Chiaretta.

On the very same day that the queen
was delivered, it chanced that there were
born in the stable-yard three black mon-

grel pups, two dogs and a bitch, which, by some strange freak, had white stars on their foreheads and bore round their necks traces of a gorget. This coming to the knowledge of the two sisters, they took the pups away from the dam and brought them to the queen-mother, and with humble salutations said to her: 'We know, madam, that your highness has little love for our sister, and quite justly; for she is of humble stock, and it is not seemly that your son and our king should have mated with such an one. Hence, knowing the mind you have towards her, we have brought you here three mongrel pups, which, as you will see, were born with a star on their foreheads, and you can deal with them as you list.' At these words the queen-mother was much pleased, divining well their evil intent, and she contrived to bring to her daughter-in-law, who as yet had not seen the children she had borne, the three whelps, telling her at the same time they were her own offspring. And for the better hiding of this trick the wicked old woman bade the midwife to tell the same story to the queen. So when she herself and the two sisters and the midwife returned to the chamber, they presented to the queen the three mongrel whelps, saying, 'See, O queen, the fruit of your womb! Cherish it well, so that the king, when he comes back, may rejoice in the fair gift you have made him.' And with these words the midwife put the mongrels by her side, consoling her and telling her that such mischances as hers happened now and then to persons of high estate.

These wicked women having carried out this barbarous work, it only remained for them to contrive a cruel death for the three lovely children of the queen. But God mercifully held them back from soiling their hands with the blood of their kin. They made a box, which they waxed within, and, having put the children therein, they closed it and cast it into the river to be borne away by the

stream. But God in His justice would
not allow these innocents to suffer. As
the box floated along it was espied by
a certain miller named Marmiato, who
haled it out and opened it, and found
within three smiling children. Seeing
how fair and graceful they were, he
deemed them to be the children of some
noble lady who, to hide her shame, had
committed this crime. Having taken
home the box he said to his wife, who
was called Gordiana, ' See here, wife,
what I have found in the river ; it is a
present for you.' Gordiana received the
children joyfully, and brought them up
as if they had been her own, giving to
one the name of Acquirino, to another
Fluvio—as they had been found in the
river—and to the girl that of Serena.

Ancilotto, when he came back from
his journey, was in high spirits, for he
fully expected to find on his return that
Chiaretta had fulfilled her pledge and
given him the three fair children as she
had promised ; but the issue was not

what he hoped, for the cunning queen-
mother, when she saw her son drawing
near, went to meet him, and told him
that the wife he prized so highly had
given him, instead of three children, three
mongrel dogs. And having brought him
into the chamber of the unfortunate Chiaretta, she showed him the pups which
were lying beside her. The queen began to weep bitterly and to deny that
the dogs were her offspring, but her
wicked sisters came and declared that
everything the old mother had said was
the truth. The king when he heard
this was greatly disturbed, and fell to
the ground grief-stricken. After he had
come to himself he could scarce believe
such thing could be; but at last he gave
ear to his mother's false tale. But Chiaretta's dignity and sweetness, and the
patience with which she bore the insults
of the courtiers, won him over to spare
her life, and to sentence her to be kept
in a cell under the place where the cook-
ing pots and pans were washed, and to

be fed on the garbage which was swept
off the dirty sink.

While the unhappy queen passed her
life in this filthy wise, feeding upon carrion, Gordiana, the wife of the miller
Marmiato, gave birth to a son who was
christened Borghino and brought up with
the three foundlings.   When Gordiana
went to cut the hair of these there often
fell out of it many precious stones and
great white pearls ; so with these riches
Marmiato was able to give over the
humble calling of a miller, and to live
with his wife and the four children a
life of ease and delicacy.   But when the
three foundlings had come to years of
discretion they learned by chance that
they were not the children of Marmiato
and Gordiana, but had been found float-
ing in a box on the river.   As soon as
they knew this they became very unhappy, and resolved to go their way and
try their fortune elsewhere, much to the
chagrin of their foster-parents, who saw
they would no longer enjoy the rich har-

vest of jewels which was wont to fall
from the children's locks and starry foreheads. The brothers and their sister
having left Marmiato the miller and
Gordiana, they all wandered about for
some days, and at last came by chance
to Provino, the city of Ancilotto their
father, where they hired a house and
lived together, maintaining themselves
by selling the jewels which still fell out
of their hair. One day the king, who
was riding into the country with some
of his courtiers, chanced to pass the
house where the three were living, and
they, as soon as they heard the king was
coming, ran down the steps and stood
bareheaded to give him a respectful sal-
utation. They had never seen Ancilotto, so his face was unknown to them.
The king, whose eyes were as keen as
a hawk's, looked at them steadily, and
remarked that on their foreheads there
was something like a golden star, and
immediately his heart was filled with
strong passion, and he felt that they

might prove to be his children. He
stopped and said to them: 'Who are
you, and from whence do you come?'
And they answered humbly, 'We are
poor strangers who have come to dwell
in this your city.' Then said Ancilotto,
'I am greatly pleased; and what are you
called?' Whereupon they replied that
one was named Acquirino, and the other
Fluvio, and the sister, Serena. The
king then bade them to dinner with him
next day; and the young people, though
they were almost overcome by his gracious invitation, did not venture to decline it. When Ancilotto returned to the
palace he said to his mother: 'Madam,
when I was abroad to-day I came by
chance upon two handsome youths and a
lovely maiden, who, as they had golden
stars on their foreheads, must be I think
the children promised to me by Queen
Chiaretta.'

The wicked old woman smiled at the
king's words, making believe they were
but fancy, but within she felt as if a dag-

ger had smitten her heart. Then she
bade them summon the midwife who had
been present at the birth, and said to her
in private, 'Good gossip, do you not
know that the king's children, so far from
being dead as we hoped, are alive, and
are grown up as beautiful as the day?'
'How can this be?' replied the woman;
'were they not drowned in the river?
Who has told you this?' The queen-
mother answered: 'From what I gather
from the words of the king I am almost
sure they are alive. We must be up
and doing at once, for we are in great
danger.' 'Do not be alarmed, madam,'
said the midwife, 'I have in mind a plan
by which we can now assuredly compass
the destruction of all the three.'

The midwife went out, and immediately found her way to the house of
the king's children, and, finding Serena
alone, she saluted her and talked of many
things. After she had held a long discourse with her, she said, 'My daughter,
I am curious to know if you have in your

house any water which can dance.' Serena, somewhat surprised at this question,
answered that she had not any. 'Ah,
my daughter,' said the gossip, 'what delights you would enjoy if you had some
of it! and if you could bathe your face
in it you would become more beautiful
even than you are now.' Said the girl,
with her curiosity aroused, 'And how can
I get it?' 'Have you not brothers?'
the gossip asked. 'Send them to fetch
it; they will easily find it, for it is to be
had not far from these parts.' And with
these words she departed. After a little
Acquirino and Fluvio came back, and at
once Serena began to beseech them that
they would do their best, for the love they
bore her, to get for her some of the wonderful dancing water; but they laughed
at her request as a silly fancy, and refused
to go on a fool's errand, seeing that no
one could say where it was to be found.
However, persuaded at last by the petition of their sister, whom they loved very
dearly, they departed together to do her

bidding, taking with them a phial to hold the precious water. When they had gone several miles they came to a fountain out of which a snow-white dove was drinking, and they were amazed when the bird spoke to them these words: 'What seek ye, young men?' To this Fluvio answered, 'We seek the precious dancing water.' 'Wretched youths,' said the dove, 'who sends you on such a quest as this?' 'We want it for our sister,' said Fluvio. 'Then you will surely meet your deaths,' said the dove, 'for the water you are in search of is guarded by many fierce beasts and poisonous dragons, who will certainly devour you; but if you must needs have some of it, leave the task to me, for I will surely bring it back to you;' and having taken the phial the dove flew away out of sight.

Acquirino and Fluvio awaited her return with the greatest anxiety, and at last she came in sight, bearing the phial filled with the magic water. They took it

from her, and, having thanked her for the
great service she had rendered them, returned to their sister and gave her the
water, exhorting her never to impose
such another task upon them, because
they had nearly met their deaths in at-
tempting it.   A short time after this the
king again met the two brothers and said
to them : ' Why did you not come to dine
with me after accepting my invitation ? '
' Gracious majesty,' they answered with
profound respect, ' a pressing errand
called us away from home.'   Then said
the king, ' To-morrow I shall expect to
see you without fail.'   The youths having made their apology, the king returned to the palace, where he met his
mother and told her he had once more
seen the youths with the stars on their
foreheads.   Again the queen-mother was
greatly perplexed, and again she bade
them summon the midwife, to whom she
secretly told all she had heard, and at the
same time begged her to find a way out
of the danger.   The gossip bade her take

courage, for she would so plan this time that they would be seen no more. The midwife went again to seek Serena, whom she found alone, and asked her whether she had got any of the dancing water. 'I have it,' the girl replied, 'but the winning of it nearly caused the death of my brothers.' 'The water is fair enough,' said the woman, 'but you ought to have likewise the singing apple. You never saw fruit so fair to look upon, or listened to music so sweet as that which it discourses.' 'But how shall I get it?' said Serena; 'for my brothers will never go in search of it, seeing that in their last venture they were more in peril of death than in hope of life.' 'But they won the dancing water for you,' said the woman, 'and they are still alive; they will get for you the singing apple just as harmlessly;' and, having spoken, she went her way.

Scarcely had the midwife gone when Acquirino and Fluvio came in, and again Serena cried out to them: 'Oh, my

brothers! I hear now of another wonder,
more beautiful far than the dancing water.
It is the singing apple, and if I cannot
have it I shall die of vexation.'   When
Acquirino and Fluvio heard these words
they chid her sharply, affirming that for
her sake they were reluctant to brave
again the risk of death.   But she did
not cease her prayers, and she wept and
sobbed so sorely that the brothers, seeing that this new desire of hers came
from her inmost soul, again gave way
and agreed to satisfy it at whatever risk.
They mounted and rode on till they
came to an inn, and demanded of the
host whether he could let them know
where was to be found the apple which
sang so sweetly.   He told them he knew
thereof, and warned them of the perils
which lay in the path of anyone bold
enough to seek to pluck it.   'It grows,'
he said, 'in the midst of a fair garden,
and is watched day and night by a poisonous beast which kills without fail all those
who come nigh to the tree.'   'What then

would you counsel us to do?' said the
youths; 'for we are set upon plucking
the apple at all cost.' 'If you will carry
out my behests,' said the host, 'you
may pluck the apple without fear of the
poisonous beast or of death. You must
take this robe, which, as you see, is all
covered with mirrors, and one of you
must put it on, and thus attired enter
the garden, the door of which will be
found unfastened; but the other must
bide without and be careful not to let
himself be seen. And the beast forthwith will make for the one who enters,
and, seeing an exact similitude of himself reflected by the mirrors, will fall
down to the ground, and then the ad-
venturer may go quickly up to the tree
and pluck tenderly the singing apple and
without once looking behind him quit
the garden.' The young men thanked
their host courteously, and observed all
his directions so faithfully that they won
the apple without mischance, and carried
it back to Serena, and again besought

her no more to compel them to run into
such danger.   Thus for a second time
they failed to keep their engagement
with the king, who, meeting them again
a few days afterwards, said : 'For what
reason have you once more disobeyed
my commands and failed to come and
dine with me?'   Fluvio answered as before that some weighty matters of business had intervened and kept them from
doing themselves the great honour the
king had proposed for them.   Then said
the king, 'You must come to-morrow,
and see that you fail not.'   Acquirino
promised obedience, and the king returned to his palace, where he met his
mother and told her he had again seen
the two youths, that he was more firmly
persuaded than ever that they must be
the children promised him by Chiaretta,
and that he would feel no rest till they
should have eaten at his table.   The
queen-mother when she heard that they
yet lived was in sore terror, doubting not
that her fraud had been discovered, and

thus, struck with grief and terror, she
sent for the midwife and said to her: 'I
surely thought the children were dead
by this time, and that we should hear
no more of them; but they are alive,
and we stand in peril of death. Look
therefore to our affair; otherwise we shall
be lost.' 'Noble lady,' said the midwife, 'take heart. This time I will work
their bane without fail, and you will
bless me therefor, seeing that they will
trouble you no longer;' and the woman,
full of rage at her failure, again repaired
to the house of Serena, where she found
the girl alone. With crafty speech she
inquired of Serena whether she had indeed got the singing apple, and the girl
made answer that she had. Then said
the cunning woman: 'Ah, my daughter,
you must think that you have nothing
at all if you do not get one thing more,
the most beautiful, the most graceful
thing in the world.' 'Good mother,
what may this fair thing be?' said the
girl. The old woman replied: 'It is

the beautiful green bird, my child, which
talks night and day, and speaks words
of marvellous wisdom. If you had it in
your keeping you might indeed call yourself happy;' and, having thus spoken,
she went her way.

Acquirino and Fluvio came in almost
directly after she was gone, and Serena
forthwith began to beg them to do her
one last favour, whereupon they asked
her what might be this boon which she
desired. She answered that she wanted
the beautiful green bird. Fluvio, who
had plucked the apple guarded by the
venomous beast, was still haunted by
the peril of his adventure, and refused
to go in quest of the bird. Acquirino,
though for a long time he too turned a
deaf ear, was finally moved by the brotherly love he felt and by the hot tears of
grief which Serena shed, and determined
to satisfy her wish. Fluvio also agreed
to accompany him, and, having mounted
their horses, they rode for several days,
until at last they came into a flowery

green meadow, in the midst of which
stood a lofty tree surrounded with marble statues which mocked life by their
marvellous workmanship. Through the
meadow there ran a little stream, and up
in the tall tree lived the beautiful green
bird, which hopped about from bough
to bough in lively fashion, uttering the
while words which seemed rather divine
than human. The young men dismounted from their palfreys, which they
left to graze at will, and went close to
the marble statues· to examine them ;
but, as soon as they touched these, they
themselves were turned into marble as
they stood.

Now Serena, when for several months
she had anxiously looked for the return
of her dear brothers Acquirino and Fluvio, began to despair and to fear she
would never see them more, and, overcome with grief at their unhappy fate,
she resolved to try her own fortune. So
she mounted a mettlesome horse, and
rode on and on till she came to the fair

meadow where the green bird was hopping about on the tall tree and softly talking. There the first things she saw was her brothers' horses, which were grazing on the turf, and, casting her eyes upon the statues, she saw that two of them must be Acquirino and Fluvio, for the unhappy youths, though turned into marble, retained their features exactly as in life. Serena dismounted, and going softly up to the tree she laid hands on the green bird from behind, and he, finding himself a prisoner, besought her to let him go, and promised that at the right time and place he would remember her. But Serena answered that first of all he must restore her brothers to their former state, upon which the bird replied: ' Look then under my left wing, and there you will find a feather much greener than any of the others and marked with yellow. Pluck it out and touch with it the eyes of the statues, and then your brothers will return to flesh and blood.' Serena raised the wing, and found the feather, and did as the bird had directed, and the statues of Acquirino and Fluvio at once became living men and embraced their sister joyfully.

This wonder being accomplished, the bird again besought Serena to give him his liberty, promising that if she would grant his prayer he would come to her aid, whenever she might call upon him ; but Serena was not to be thus cajoled, and declared that before she would let him go free he must help them to find their father and mother, and that until he had accomplished this task he must be her prisoner.

There had already arisen some dispute amongst the three as to who should have the bird in keeping, but in the end they settled that it should be left in charge of Serena, who tended it with great care and watched over it. The affair having come to this happy issue, they mounted their horses and rode home. Meantime Ancilotto had often passed by their house, and finding it empty was much astonished, and inquired of the neighbours what had become of them; but all he could learn was that nothing had been seen of them for many days. They had not been back long before the king again rode by, and, catching sight of them, asked how it was that nothing had been seen of them for so long, and why they had disregarded his commands so often. Acquirino answered with deep respect that some amazing troubles and adventures had befallen them, and that if they had not presented themselves at the palace before his majesty as he had desired it was through no want of reverence. They were all anxious to amend their conduct in the future.

The king, when he heard they had been in tribulation, was moved to pity, and bade them all accompany him back to the palace to dinner; but before they set forth Acquirino filled secretly a phial with the dancing water, Fluvio took the singing apple, and Serena the talking bird, and they rode back with the king

and joyously entered the palace with him
and sat down at the royal table. It
chanced that the queen-mother and also
the two sisters of Chiaretta marked them
as they passed, and observing the beauty
of the maiden and the handsome bright-
eyed youths, they were filled with dread
and suspicion as to who they might be.
When the royal banquet had come to
an end, Acquirino said to the king : ' May
it please your majesty that, before we
take our leave, we should show your
majesty some marvels which may delight
you ; ' and with these words he poured
into a silver tazza some of the dancing
water, while Fluvio put his hand into his
bosom and drew therefrom the singing
apple, which he placed beside the water.
Serena also brought out the talking bird,
and set it on the table. Immediately the
apple began to sing most sweetly, and
the wonderful water to dance, so that the
king and all the courtiers were delighted
and laughed aloud with pleasure ; but
the queen-mother and the wicked sisters

were smitten with dire dismay, for they felt that their doom was near.

At last, when the apple and the water had ceased to sing and dance, the bird opened its mouth and said: 'O sacred majesty! what doom should be dealt to those who once plotted death against two brothers and a sister?' Then the cunning queen-mother, scheming to excuse herself, cried out: 'No lighter doom than death by burning;' and in this condemnation all those who were present agreed. To answer her the singing apple and the dancing water said straightway: 'Ah, false and cruel woman! your own tongue has doomed yourself, and those wicked and envious sisters of the queen, and the vile midwife, to this horrible death.'

When the king heard these words his heart grew cold with terror; but before he could speak the talking bird began and said: 'O sacred majesty! these are the three children you longed for, your children who bear the star on their foreheads; and their innocent mother, is she

not to this day kept a prisoner under the
filthy scullery?' Then the king saw
clearly how he had been tricked, and gave
order that the unhappy Chiaretta should
be taken out of her noisome prison and
robed once more in her royal garments.
As soon as this had been done, she was
brought into the presence of the king and
of his court; and though she had for so
long time suffered such cruel usage, she
retained all her former loveliness. Then
the talking bird related the strange his-
tory from beginning to end, and the king,
when he knew it all, embraced tenderly
Chiaretta and their three children; but
the dancing water and the singing apple
and the talking bird, having been set at
liberty, disappeared straightway.

The next day the king commanded to
be lighted in the centre of the market
a huge fire, into which he caused to be
thrown, without pity, his mother and the
two sisters of Chiaretta and the midwife,
so that in the presence of everybody they
might be burnt to death. And Anci-

lotto lived happily many years with his beloved wife and his beautiful children, and, having chosen for Serena an honourable husband, he left his two sons the heirs of his kingdom.

Lodovica's story gave great delight to all the ladies, and the Signora, having commanded her to supplement it in due order, she propounded the following enigma :

> When Sol pours down his fiercest heat,
> High on Gheraldo's lofty seat,
> A wight I marked, with roguish eye,
> Shut fast within a closure high.
> All through the day he prates and talks,
> And clad in robes of emerald walks.
> I've told you all except his name,
> And that from your own wit I claim.

Many were the interpretations put upon this enigma, but no one came near to the mark save the charming Isabella, who, greatly pleased with herself, said in a merry tone: "There is no other possible signification of Lodovica's enigma

except to name the parroquet, which
lives within a cage, the closure, and has
plumage green as emerald, and talks all
day long." The clever solution of the
riddle pleased everybody except Lodovica, who had flattered herself that no
one would be clever enough to solve it,
and who now became almost dumb with
vexation. A little later, when the flush
of anger had faded somewhat from her
cheek, she turned to Isabella, whose turn
it was to tell the fourth story, and said:
"I am vexed, Isabella, not from envy of
you, as the teller of the next story, but
because I feel myself inferior to those
other companions of yours who have had
to give the solution of their riddles, the
company not being able to solve them;
whereas mine was guessed at once. Be
assured, however, that if I can give you
a Roland for your Oliver, I will not be
caught napping."[1] Isabella answered
quickly, "You will do well, Signora Lo-

---

[1] Orig., *che se io potrò rendervi il contra cambio non
starò a dormire.*

dovica, but —" Here the Signora, who
saw that the contention was like to grow
warm between the two, commanded Isabella to go on at once with her story,
which, with a smile, she began to tell as
follows.

THE FOURTH FABLE.

*Nerino, the son of Gallese, King of Portugal,
becoming enamoured of Genobbia, wife of Messer Raimondo Brunello, a physician, has his
will of her and carries her with him to Portugal, while Messer Raimondo dies of grief.*

I MUST tell you, charming
ladies, that there are very many
men who, because they have
consumed a great part of their
time over the study of letters, are persuaded that they are mighty wise, whereas
in truth they know little or nothing.
And while men of this sort think they
are marking their foreheads with lines of
wisdom, they too often only scoop out
their own eyes,[1] which thing happened

---

[1] Orig., *credonsi signare il fronte à se stessi cavano
gli occhi.*

to a certain physician, greatly skilled in his calling, for he, while he deemed he was about to put a cheat upon another, was himself most ignominiously duped, to his own great injury, all of which you will learn from the fable which I will presently tell you.

Gallese, King of Portugal, had a son whose name was Nerino, and in the bringing up of this boy he followed such a course that up to the time when he reached his eighteenth year Nerino had never once cast eyes upon a woman except his mother and the nurse who had the care of him. Wherefore when he had come to full age the king determined to send him to pursue his studies in the university of Padua, so that he might get a knowledge of Latin letters and of the tongue and manners of the Italians as well. And the plan which he had devised he duly carried out. When the young Nerino. had come to Padua, he soon acquired the friendship of many of the scholars, and every day these would

come to pay their respects to him, one of
the above named being a certain Messer
Raimondo Brunello, a physician.   It
chanced one day, as Nerino and this friend
of his were conversing now about this
thing and now about that, they engaged
(as is the manner of sprightly youths)
in a discourse anent the beauty of women,
and on this subject the former took one
view and the latter another.   But Nerino,
though he had never in times past cast
eyes upon any woman save his mother
and his nurse, declared with some heat
that in his reckoning there could not be
found in all the world any lady who
should be more beautiful, more graceful,
and more exquisite, than was his own
mother.   And when, by way of putting
this speech of his to the test, they brought
divers ladies to his notice, he still declared that in comparison to his mother
they were little better than carrion.

Now Messer Raimondo had to wife
a lady who was one of the fairest nature
ever created, and when he listened to

this chattering he settled his gorget and said : ' Signor Nerino, I happen to have seen a certain lady who is of such great loveliness that when you shall have beheld her I think it probable you will judge her to be not less but more beautiful than your mother.' To this speech Nerino made answer that he could not believe there could be any woman more lovely than his mother, but at the same time it would give him great pleasure to look upon this one. Whereupon Messer Raimondo said ; ' Whenever it shall please you to behold her I will gladly point her out to you.' Nerino replied : ' I am much pleased at what you propose, and I shall ever be obliged to you.' Then Messer Raimondo said at once : ' Since it will give you pleasure to see her, take care to be present in the Church of the Duomo to-morrow morning, for there I promise you that you shall have sight of her.'

When he had returned to his house, Messer Raimondo said to his wife : ' To-

morrow morning see that you rise be-
times, and deck carefully your head, and
make yourself seem as fair as you can,
and put on the most sumptuous raiment
you possess, for I have a mind that you
should go to the Duomo at the hour of
high mass to hear the office.' Genobbia
(for this was the name of Messer Raimondo's wife), not being in the habit of
going now hither now thither, but rather
to pass all her time at home over her
sewing and broidery work, was much
astonished at these words; but, seeing
that her husband's command fell in well
with her own desire, she did all she was
directed to do, and set herself so well in
order and decked herself so featly that
she looked more like a goddess than like
a mortal woman. And when Genobbia,
following the command which her husband had laid upon her, had entered into
the holy fane, there came thither likewise Nerino, the son of the king, and
when he had looked upon her he found
that she was exceedingly fair. When the

lady had gone her way, Messer Raimondo came upon the scene, and having
gone up to Nerino spake thus: ' Now
how does that lady who is just gone out
of the church please you? Does she
seem to you to be one who ought to be
compared with any other? Say, is she
not more beautiful than your mother?'
' Of a truth,' replied Nerino, ' she is
fair, and nature could not possibly make
aught that is fairer; but tell me of your
courtesy of whom is she the wife, and
where does she dwell?' But to this
query Messer Raimondo did not answer
so as to humour Nerino's wish, forasmuch as he had no mind to give him
the clue he sought. Then said Nerino,
' My good Messer Raimondo, though
you may not be willing to tell me who
she is and where she dwells, at least you
might do me such good office as to let
me see her once more.' 'This I will do
willingly,' answered Messer Raimondo.
' To-morrow come here again into the
church, and I will so bring it to pass

that you shall see her as you have seen her to-day.'

When Messer Raimondo had gone back to his house, he said to his wife, 'Genobbia, see that you attire yourself to-morrow; for I wish that you should go to the mass in the Duomo, and if hitherto you have ever made yourself look beautiful or have arrayed yourself sumptuously, see that you do the same to-morrow.' When she heard this, Genobbia (as on the former occasion) was greatly astonished, but since the command of her husband pointed to this matter, she did everything even as he had ordered. When the morrow came, Genobbia, sumptuously clothed and adorned more richly than was her wont, betook herself to the church, and in a very short time Nerino came likewise. He, when he saw how very fair she was, was inflamed by love of her more ardently than ever man had burned for woman before, and, when Messer Raimondo arrived, begged him to tell straightway

what might be the name of this lady who
seemed in his eyes to be so marvellously
beautiful. But Messer Raimondo, making excuse that he was greatly pressed for
time to give to his own affairs, was in no
humour to thus inform Nerino on the
spot, and was rather disposed to leave
the galliard to stew for a time in his own
fat; so he went his way in high spirits.
Whereupon Nerino, with his temper
somewhat ruffled by the mean account
in which Messer Raimondo seemed to
hold him, spake thus to himself: 'Aha!
you are not willing that I should have
an inkling as to who she is and where she
lives, but I will know what I want to know
in spite of you.'

After he had left the church, Nerino
waited outside until such time as the fair
dame should likewise issue forth, and
then, having given her a modest obeisance
with a smiling countenance, he went with
her as far as her home. Now, as soon
as Nerino had got to know clearly the
house where she dwelt, he began to cast

amorous eyes upon her, and never a day
passed on which he would not pass up
and down ten times in front of her window.   Wherefore, having a great desire
to hold converse with her, he set about
considering what course he should follow
in order to keep unsullied the honour of
the lady, and at the same time to attain
his own end.   But, having pondered over
the affair, and looked at it on every side
without lighting upon any course which
seemed to promise security, he at last,
after a mighty amount of imagining, determined to make the acquaintance of an
old woman who lived in a house opposite
to that occupied by Genobbia.   After
having sent to her certain presents, and
settled and confirmed the compact between them, he went secretly into the old
woman's lodging, in which there was a
certain window overlooking the hall of
Genobbia's house, where he might stand
and gaze at his good convenience at the
lady as she went up and down about the
house ; at the same time, he had no wish

to divulge himself, and thereby give her any pretext for withdrawing herself from his sight.   Nerino, having spent one day after another in these amorous glances, at last found himself no longer able to resist the burning desire within him which consumed his very heart ; so he made up his mind to write a letter and to throw it down into her lodging at a certain time when he should judge her husband to be away from home.   And several times he wrote letters as he had planned and threw them down to her.

But Genobbia without reading the billet she picked up, cast it into the fire, and it was burnt.   After she had done this several times, on a certain day it came into her mind to break open one of the notes and see what might be written therein.   When she had broken the seal and marked that the writer was no other than Nerino, the son of the King of Portugal, who declared thereby his fervent love of her, she was at first wellnigh confounded, but after a little when she had

called to mind the poor cheer she en-
joyed in her husband's house, she
plucked· up heart and began to look
kindly upon Nerino.   At last, having
come to an agreement with him, she
found means to bring him into the house,
when the youth laid before her the story
of the ardent love he bore her, and of
the torments he endured every day on
her account, and in like manner the way
by which his passion for her had been
kindled.   Wherefore the lady, who was
alike lovely and kind-hearted and complaisant, felt herself in no humour to re-
ject his suit.   And while the two thus
foregathered, happy in the consciousness
of mutual love and indulging in amorous
discourse, lo and behold! Messer Raimondo knocked suddenly at the door.
When Genobbia heard this she bade
Nerino go straightway and lie down on
the bed, and to let down the curtains, and
to remain there until such time as her
husband should be once more gone out.
The husband came in, and having taken

divers trifles of which he had need, went
away without giving heed to aught besides, and a little later Nerino followed
him.

On the following day, when it happened that Nerino was walking up and
down the piazza, Messer Raimondo by
chance went that way, to whom Nerino
made known by sign that he wanted to
have a word with him. Wherefore, having
approached him, he spake thus : 'Signor,
have I not a good bit of news to tell you?'
'And what may it be?' replied Messer
Raimondo. 'Do I not know,' said Nerino,
'the house where dwells that beautiful
lady? and have I not had some delightful intercourse with her? But because
her husband came home unexpectedly
she hid me in the bed, and drew the
curtains for fear that he should see me ;
however, he soon went out again.' 'Is it
possible?' said Messer Raimondo. 'Possible !' answered Nerino, 'it is more than
possible — it is a fact. Never in all my
life have I seen so delightful, so sweet a

lady as she. If by any chance, signor, you should meet her, I beg you to speak a good word on my behalf, and to entreat her to keep me in her good graces.' Messer Raimondo, having promised to do what the youth asked him, went his way with ill will in his heart. But before he left Nerino he said, ' And do you propose to go in search of your good fortune again?' To this Nerino replied, ' Return! what should one do in such case?' Then Messer Raimondo went back to his house, and was careful to let drop no word in his wife's presence, but to wait for the time when she and Nerino should again come together.

When the next day had come Nerino once more stole to a meeting with Genobbia, and while they were in the midst of their amorous delights and pleasant converse the husband came back to the house, but the lady quickly hid Nerino in a chest in front of which she heaped a lot of clothes from which she had been ripping the wadding to keep them from de-

.struction by insects. The husband, making believe to search for certain things, turned the house upside down, and pried even into the bed, but, finding nothing of the sort he looked for, went about his business with his mind more at ease.

Very soon Nerino also departed, and afterwards, chancing to meet Messer Raimondo, he thus addressed him : 'Signor doctor, what would you say if you heard I had paid another visit to my charming lady, and that envious fortune broke in upon our pleasure, seeing that the husband again arrived and spoilt all our sport?' 'And what did you then?' said Messer Raimondo. 'She straightway opened a chest,' said Nerino, 'and put me therein, and in front of the chest she piled up a heap of clothes which she was working at in order to preserve them from moth, and after he had turned the bed upside down more than once without finding aught, he went away.' What tortures Messer Raimondo must have suffered when he listened to these words I leave to the judgment of any who may know the humours of love.

Now Nerino had given to Genobbia a very fine and precious diamond, within the golden setting of which was engraved his name and his likeness. The very next day, when Messer Raimondo had gone to see to his affairs, the lady once more let Nerino into the house, and while they were taking their pleasure and talking pleasantly together, behold! the husband again came back to the house. But the crafty Genobbia, as soon as she remarked his coming, immediately opened a large wardrobe which stood in her chamber, and hid Nerino therein. Almost immediately Messer Raimondo entered the chamber, pretending as before that he was in search of certain things he wanted, and in quest thereof he turned the room upside down. But, finding nothing either in the bed or in the chest, like a man out of his wits he took fire and strewed it in the four corners of the chamber, with the intention of burning the place and all that it contained.

Now the party walls and the wooden framing of the apartment soon caught fire, whereupon Genobbia, turning to her husband, said : 'What is this you are doing, husband ? Surely you must be gone mad. Still, if you wish to burn up the room, burn it as you will, but by my faith I will not have you burn this wardrobe, wherein are all the papers relating to my dowry.' So, having summoned four strong porters, she bade them carry the wardrobe out of the house and bear it into the neighboring house which belonged to the old woman. Then she opened the wardrobe secretly when no one was by and returned to her own house. Messer Raimondo, now like one out of his mind, still kept a sharp watch to see whether anybody who ought not to have been there might be driven out of hiding by the conflagration, but he met with nothing save the smoke, which was becoming insufferable, and the fierce flames which were consuming the house. And by this time all the neighbors had gathered together to put out the fire, and so well and heartily did they work that in time it was extinguished.

On the following day, as Nerino was sallying forth towards the fields in the valley, he met Messer Raimondo, and after giving him a salute, said to him: 'Aha, my gentleman! I have got a piece of news to tell you which ought to please you mightily.' 'And what may this news be?' said Messer Raimondo. 'I have just made my escape,' said Nerino, 'from the most frightful peril that ever man came out of without loss of his life. I had gone to the house of my lovely mistress, and while I was spending the time with her in all manner of delightful dallying her husband once more broke in upon our content, and after he had turned the house upside down, lighted some fire, and this he scattered about in the four corners of the room and burnt up all the chattels that were about.' 'And you,' said Messer Raimondo, 'where were you the while?' Then answered Nerino,

' I was hidden in a wardrobe which she caused to be taken out of the house.' And when Messer Raimondo heard this, and clearly understood all which Nerino told him to be the truth, he was like to die of grief and passion. Nevertheless, he did not dare to let his secret be known, because he was determined still to catch him in the act. Wherefore he said to him, 'And are you bent upon going thither again, Signor Nerino?' to which Nerino made answer, ' Seeing that I have come safely out of the fire, what else is there for me to fear?' And, letting pass any further remarks of this sort, Messer Raimondo begged Nerino that he would do him the honour of dining with him on the morrow; which civility the young man willingly accepted.

When the next day had come, Messer Raimondo bade assemble at his house all his own relations and his wife's as well, and prepared for their entertainment a rich and magnificent repast — not in the house which had been half consumed by fire, but in another. He gave directions to his wife, moreover, that she also should be present, not to sit at table as a guest, but to keep herself out of sight, and see to the ordering of aught which might be required for the banquet. As soon as all the kinsfolk had assembled, and the young Nerino as well, they were bidden take their places at the board, and as the feast went on Messer Raimondo tried his best with his charlatan science to make Nerino drunk, in order to be able to work his will upon him. Having several times handed to the youth a glass of malvoisie wine, which he never failed to empty, Messer Raimondo said to him: ' Now, Signor Nerino, cannot you tell to these kinsfolk of mine some little jest which may make them laugh?' The luckless Nerino, who had no inkling that Genobbia was Messer Raimondo's wife, began to tell the story of his adventures, keeping back, however, the names of all concerned.

It chanced at this moment that one of

the servants went into the room apart
where Genobbia was, and said to her:
' Madonna, if only you were now hidden
in some corner of the feasting-room, you
would hear told the finest story you ever
heard in your life. I pray you go in
quick.' And, having stolen into a corner, she knew that the voice of the story-
teller belonged to Nerino her lover, and
that the tale he was giving to the company concerned himself and her as well.
Whereupon this prudent and sharp-
witted dame took the diamond which
Nerino had given her, and, having placed
it in a cup filled with a very dainty drink,
she said to a servant, ' Take this cup and
give it to Signor Nerino, and tell him to
drink it off forthwith, that he may tell
his story the better.' The servant took
the cup, and placed it on the table,
whereupon Nerino gave sign that he
wished to drink therefrom ; so the servant
said to him, ' Take this cup, signor, so
that you may tell your story the better.'

Nerino took the cup and forthwith

drank all the wine therein, when, seeing
and recognizing the diamond which lay
at the bottom, he let it pass into his
mouth. Then making pretence of rins-
ing his teeth, he drew forth the ring and
put it on his finger. As soon as he was
well assured that the fair lady about
whom he was telling his story was the wife
of Messer Raimondo, he had no mind to
say more, and when Messer Raimondo
and his kinsfolk began to urge him to
bring the tale which he had begun to an
end, he replied, 'And then and there the
cock crowed and the day broke, so I
awoke from my sleep and heard nothing
more.' Messer Raimondo's kinsmen,
having listened to Nerino's story, and up
to this time believed all he had said about
the lady to be the truth, now imagined
that both their host and the young man
were drunk.

After several days had passed it happened that Nerino met Messer Raimondo, and feigning not to know that he
was the husband of Genobbia, told him

that within the space of two days he
would take his departure, because his
father had written to him to bid him
without fail to return to his own country.   Whereupon Messer Raimondo
wished him good speed for his journey.
Nerino, having come to a private under-
standing with Genobbia, carried her off
with him and fled to Portugal, where
they long lived a gay life together; but
Messer Raimondo, when he went back
to his house and found that his wife was
gone, was stricken with despair, and died
in the course of a few days.

Isabella's fable pleased the ladies and
gentlemen equally well, and they rejoiced especially that Messer Raimondo
himself proved to be the cause of his
own misfortune, and that the thing
which he had courted had really fallen
upon him.   And when the Signora
marked that this discourse was come to
an end, she gave the sign to Isabella to
finish her task in due order, and she,
in no wise neglectful of the Signora's

command, gave the enigma which follows:

In the middle of the night,
Rises one with beard bedight.
Though no astrologer he be,
He marks the hours which pass and flee.
He wears a crown, although no king;
No priest, yet he the hour doth sing,
Though spurred at heel he is no knight;
No wife he calls his own by right,
Yet children many round him dwell.
Sharp wits you need this thing to tell.

Here the cleverly-devised enigma of
Isabella came to an end, and although
the various listeners went casting about
in various directions, no one hit upon
the exact truth except the somewhat
haughty Lodovica, who, mindful of the
slight which had of late been put upon
her, rose to her feet and spake thus:
"The enigma which our sister has set
us to guess means nothing else than
the cock, which is on the alert to crow
while it is yet night; which wears a
beard and has knowledge of the passage

of time, although he is no astrologer.
He bears a crest instead of a crown, and
is no king ; he sings the hours, yet is no
priest. Besides this, he wears spurs on
his heels ; he has no wife, and brings
up the children of others, that is to say,
the young chickens."

All the listeners commended this
solution of Isabella's skilful enigma,
especially Capello, who said : " Signora
Isabella, Lodovica has given you back
bread for your bannock,[1] seeing that a
short time ago you very cleverly declared the meaning of her enigma and
now she has mastered yours ; but for
this reason you must not harbour malice
one against another." Then Lodovica
answered promptly, " Signor Bernardo,
when the night time is come, I will pay
you back yea for yea."[2]

But in order to keep the discourse
within limits, the Signora imposed silence upon all, and, turning her face

---

[1] Orig., *pane per schiacciata.*
[2] Orig., *le renderò gnanf per gnaf.*

towards Lionora, whose turn it was to
tell the last story of the night, directed
her to begin, with due courtesy, her
fable, and the damsel, with the best
grace in the world thus began.

THE FIFTH FABLE.

Flamminio Veraldo sets out from Ostia in search
of Death, and, not finding it, meets Life instead ; this latter lets him see Fear and make
trial of Death.

ANY are the men who with all
care and diligence go searching narrowly for certain things,
which, when they have gained
them, they find of no value, and would
gladly forego, fleeing therefrom with all
speed, just as the devil flies from holy
water. This was the case of Flamminio, who, when he went seeking
Death, found Life, who made him see
Fear and make trial of Death. All of
which you will find clearly set forth in
this fable.

In Ostia, an ancient city situated no
great distance from Rome, there lived
in former days, according to the common report, a young man of a nature
rather weak and errant than stable and
prudent, whose name was Flamminio
Veraldo. He had heard it said over
and over again that there was in all the
world nothing more terrible and frightful than Death, the dark and inevitable
one, seeing that he shows pity to none,
having respect to no man, however poor
or rich he may be. Wherefore, being
filled with wonder at what he had heard,
he determined by himself to find and to
see with his own eyes what manner of
thing this might be which men called
Death. And having attired himself in
coarse garments, and taken in hand a
staff of strong cornel-wood well shod
with iron, he set forth from Ostia.
Flamminio, when he had travelled over
many miles of road, came one day into
a certain street, in the midst of which he
espied, sitting in his stall, a cobbler

making shoes and gaiters, and this cobbler, although there was lying about a
great quantity of his finished work, kept
on steadily at his task of making yet
more.

Flamminio, going up to the cobbler,
said to him, 'God be with you, good master!' and to this the cobbler replied, 'You
are right welcome here, my son.' Then
said Flamminio, 'What is this task you
labour at?' 'I labour indeed,' replied the
cobbler, 'and toil hard that I may not
languish in want.[1] Nevertheless, I am
in want, and I weary myself over making shoes.' 'Why do you thus,' said
Flamminio, 'seeing that you have so
many pairs made already? What is the
good of making more?' 'I make them,'
said the cobbler, 'to wear myself, to sell
for my own sustenance and for the sustenance of my little household, and in
order that when I become an old man I
may be able to live on the money I have
made by my handicraft.' 'And what

[1] Orig., *stento per non stentare.*

will you do next?' asked Flamminio.
'After this,' said the cobbler, 'I shall
die.' 'You will die!' cried Flamminio
in reply. 'Yes,' said the cobbler. Then
cried Flamminio, 'Oh, my good master!
can you of your own knowledge tell me
what may be this thing they call Death?'
The cobbler answered, 'Of a truth I
cannot.' 'What, have you never seen
him?' said Flamminio. To this master
cobbler made answer, 'I have never seen
him, nor have I any wish to see him
now, or to taste his quality. Moreover,
all men say that he is the strangest and
most terrible monster the world holds.'
Then Flamminio said, 'At least you will
be able of your knowledge to teach me
and tell me where he abides, because day
and night I wander over mountains and
through valleys and swamps seeking him
without ever hearing tiding as to where
he may be found?' The cobbler answered, 'I know nothing as to where
Death may dwell, nor where he is to be
found, nor what he is made of; but if

you go on with your journey somewhat farther, peradventure you will find him.'

Whereupon Flamminio, having taken his leave, parted from the cobbler, and betook himself onwards to a spot where he came upon a dense and shadowy forest, and entered therein. In a certain place he saw a peasant, who, though he had already cut a vast pile of wood for burning, went on cutting more with all his might. And when they had exchanged greetings one with another, Flamminio said to him, ' My brother, what are you going to do with so vast a heap of wood as this?' And to this the peasant made answer, ' I am preparing it to kindle fire therewith in the winter that is coming, when we shall have snow and ice and villainous mist, so that I may be able to keep warm myself and my children, and to sell whatsoever may be to spare, and to buy with the profit thereof bread and wine and clothing, and all other things which may be necessary for our daily sustenance, and thus to pass our lives until Death comes to fetch us.' 'Now, by your courtesy,' said Flamminio, 'could you tell me where this same Death is to be found?' 'Of a surety I cannot,' the peasant replied, 'seeing that I have never once seen him, nor do I know where he abides. I am here in this wood all the day long taking heed to my own affairs. Very few wayfarers come into these parts, and I know none of those who pass by.' 'What then shall I do to find him?' demanded Flamminio; and to this the peasant made answer, 'As to myself, I know not at all what to say to you nor how to direct you. I can only bid you to travel yet farther onward, and then peradventure you may meet with him.'

Having taken leave of the peasant, Flamminio departed and walked and walked until he came to a certain place where dwelt a tailor, who had a vast store of clothes upon the pegs, and a warehouse filled with all kinds of the finest garments. Said Flamminio to him, 'God be with you, my good master!'

and the tailor replied, 'And the same
good wish to you.' 'What are you going to do with all this store of fair and
sumptuous raiment, and all the noble
garments I see here? Do they all belong
to you?' Then the master tailor made
answer, 'Certain of them are my own,
some belong to the merchants, some to
the gentlefolk, and some to various people who have dealings with me.' 'But
what use can they find for so many?'
asked Flamminio. 'They wear them in
the different seasons of the year,' the
tailor answered, and showing them all
to Flamminio, he went on, 'These they
wear in the summer and these in the
winter, and these others in the seasons
which come between, clothing themselves
sometimes in one fashion and sometimes
in another.' 'And in the end what do
they do?' asked Flamminio. The tailor
answered, 'They go on in this course
until the day of their death.' Flamminio hearing the tailor speak of Death
said, 'Oh, my good master! could you

tell me where I may find this Death
you tell of?' The tailor, speaking as if
he were inflamed with anger and per-
turbed in spirit, said: 'My son, you go
about asking questions which are indeed
strange. I surely cannot tell you nor
direct you where he may abide, for I
never let my thoughts turn to him, and
it is an occasion of great offence to me
when anyone begins to talk of him.
Wherefore I bid you either to discourse
of some other matter or to go your way,
for all such talk as this displeases me
vastly.' And Flamminio, having taken
leave of the tailor, departed on his
journey.

It came to pass that Flamminio, after
he had traversed many lands, came at
last to a desert and solitary place, where
he found a hermit with his beard all
matted with dirt, and his body worn away
by the passage of the years and by fast-
ing, letting his mind concern itself only
in contemplation. Whereupon, thinking that assuredly he had at last found

Death, Flamminio thus addressed him :
' Of a truth, I am very glad to meet with
you, holy father.'   ' The sight of you is
welcome to me, my son,' the hermit replied. ' My good father,' said Flamminio,
' what do you here in this rough and
uninhabitable spot, cut off from all pleasure and from all human society ? '   ' I
pass my time,' answered the hermit, 'in
prayers and in fastings and in contemplation.'   Then Flamminio inquired, ' And
for what reason do you follow this life ? '
' Why, my son,' exclaimed the hermit,
' I do all this to serve God, to mortify
this wretched flesh of mine, to do penance
for all the offences I have wrought in the
sight of the eternal and immortal God
and of the true son of Mary, and in the
end to get salvation for my sinful soul,
so that when the hour of my death shall
come I may render it up pure of all
stain, and in the awful day of judgment,
by the grace of my Redeemer and by no
merit of my own, may make myself
worthy of that happy and glorious home

where I may taste the joys of eternal life,
to which blessedness God lead us!'
Then said Flamminio, 'Oh, my dear
father! spare a few words to tell me —
if it be not an offence to you — what
manner of thing is this Death, and after
what fashion is it made?' The holy
father answered, 'Oh, my son! trouble
not yourself to gain knowledge of this
thing you seek; for Death is a very terrible and a fearful being, and is called by
wise men the final end of all our sufferings,
a misery to the happy, a happiness to
the miserable, and the term and limit of
all worldly things. It severs friend from
friend; it separates the father from the
son, and the son from the father, the
mother from the daughter, and the daughter from the mother. It cuts the marriage bond, and finally disunites the soul
and the body, so that the body, severed
from the soul, loses all its power and becomes so putrid and of so evil a savour
that all men flee therefrom and abandon
it as a thing abominable.' 'And have

you never set eyes on him, my father?' asked Flamminio. 'Of a certainty I have never seen him,' answered the hermit. 'But can you tell me what I should do in order to see him?' asked Flamminio. 'Ah, my son!' said the hermit, 'if you are indeed so keenly set on finding him, you have only to keep going further and further on; because man, the longer the way he has journeyed through this world, the nearer he is to Death.' The young man having thanked the holy father, and received his benediction, went his way.

Then Flamminio, continuing his journey, traversed a great number of deep valleys and craggy mountains and inhospitable forests, seeing by the way many sorts of fearsome beasts, and questioning each one of these whether he was the thing called Death, and always getting in return the answer 'No.' At last, after he had passed through many lands and seen many strange things, he came to a mountain of no little magnitude,

and having climbed over this, he began
to descend into a gloomy and very deep
valley, closed in on all sides by profound
caverns. Here he saw a strange and monstrous wild beast, which made all the
valley re-echo with its roaring. 'Who
are you?' said Flamminio. 'Ho! is
it possible that you may be Death?'
To which the wild beast made answer,
'I am not Death; but pursue your way,
and soon you will find him.'

Flamminio, when he heard the answer
he had so long desired to hear, felt his
heart grow lighter. The wretched youth,
now worn out by fatigue and half dead
by reason of the long weariness and the
heavy toil he had undergone, was almost
sunk in despair, when he found himself
on the borders of a wide and spacious
plain. Having climbed to the summit
of a little hill of no great height, delightful, and covered with flowers, he looked
round about him, now here, now there,
and espied the lofty walls of a magnificent
city not far from the spot where he stood.

Whereupon he began to walk more rapidly with nimble steps, and when the shadows of evening were falling he came to one of the city gates, which was adorned with the finest white marble.   And when he had entered therein, with the leave of the keeper of the gate, the first person he met was a very old woman, full of years, with a face like that of a corpse, and a body so meagre and thin that, through her leanness, it would have been easy to count one by one every bone in her body.   Her forehead was thickly marked with wrinkles, her eyes were squinting, watery, and red, as if they had been dyed in purple, her cheeks all puckered, her lips turned inside out, her hands rough and callous ; her head was palsied, and she trembled in every limb ; she was bent almost double in her gait, and she was clad in rough and dusky clothes. Over and above this she bore by her left side a keen-edged sword, and carried in her right hand a weighty cudgel, at the end of which was wrought a point of iron

made in the shape of a triangle, and upon
this staff she would now and then lean
as if to rest herself.   On her shoulders
also she carried a large wallet, in which
she kept a great store of phials and pots
and bottles all filled with divers sorts of
liquors and unguents and plasters fitted
for the remedying of various human ail-
ments and accidents.   As soon as Flamminio's eye fell upon this toothless ugly
old harridan he was seized with the
thought that peradventure she might
prove to be that Death to find whom he
was going wandering about the world ;
so having approached her he said, ' Ah,
my good mother, may God keep and preserve you ! '   In a husky voice the old
woman made answer to him, ' And may
God keep and preserve you, my son ! '
' Tell me, my mother,' Flamminio went
on, ' whether perchance you may be the
thing men call Death ? '   The old woman
replied, ' No, I am not.   On the other
hand, I am Life ; and know, moreover,
that I happen to have with me here in

this wallet which I carry behind my back
certain liquors and unguents by the working of which I am able with ease to purify
and to cure the mortal body of man of
all the heavy diseases which afflict him,
and in the short space of a single hour
to relieve him in like manner from the
torture of any pain he may feel.'   Then
said Flamminio, ' Ah, my good mother!
can you not let me know where Death
is to be found ? '   ' And who may you
be,' asked the old woman, ' who make
this demand of me with so great persis-
tence ? '   Flamminio answered, ' I am a
youth who has already spent many days
and months and years wandering about
in search of Death, and never yet have
I been able to find in any land a man
who could tell me aught concerning him.
Wherefore, if you should happen to possess this knowledge, I beseech you of
your courtesy to let me share it, because
I am possessed by so keen a desire to look
upon him and to know what he is like,
in order that I may be certain whether

he really is the hideous and the dreadful thing which all men hold him to be.'

The old woman, when she heard the foolish request of the young man, spake thus to him : ' My son, when would it please you that I let you see Death, and judge how hideous he is, and when would you make trial of his terrors?' To this Flamminio replied : ' Ah, my mother ! keep me no longer in suspense I beg you, but let me see him now, at this present moment.' Thereupon the old woman, to satisfy his desire, made him strip himself quite naked, and, while he was taking off his garments, she worked up together certain of her drugs useful in the cure of divers diseases, and when the thing was ready, she said to him : ' Bend yourself down here, my son.' And he, in obedience to her direction, bent down. ' Now bow your head and close your eyes ; ' and Flamminio did as she bade him. Scarcely had the old woman finished her speech than she took the sharp blade which she wore by her side and with one blow struck off his head from his shoulders. Then she quickly took up the head, and, having replaced it upon the bust, she smeared it well with the plaster which she had prepared, and thereby the wound was quickly healed. But how the thing which now happened was caused I cannot say, whether it arose through the over-quickness of the old hag in putting back the head upon the shoulders, or whether she herself brought it to pass through her own craft. The head when it was joined once more to the body was put on hind part forward. Wherefore Flamminio, when he looked down upon his shoulders, his loins, and his big buttocks standing out (all of which things he had never seen hitherto), fell into such a fit of terror and dismay that, not being able to think of any place where he might be suffered to hide himself, he cried out to the old woman in a trembling dolorous voice: 'Alas, alas, my good mother! bring me back once more to my old shape; bring me back, for the love of

God, for by my faith I have never seen anything more frightful and more hideous than what I now behold. Alas! deliver me from this miserable state in which I now find myself fixed. Alas! alas! do not delay your help, my sweet good mother. Lend me your aid, for I am sure you can help me easily if you will.' The cunning old woman still kept silence, feigning all the while to know nothing of the mischance that had been wrought, and letting the wretched fellow work himself into an agony and stew in his own fat;[1] but at last, after having kept him in this plight for the space of two hours, she agreed to work the remedy he sought. So, having made him bend himself down as before, she put her hand to her sharp-cutting sword and struck off his head from his shoulders. Then she took the head in her hand, and, having placed it upon the trunk and smeared it well with her ointment, brought Flamminio back to his former condition.

---

[1] Orig., *cuocersi nel suo unto.*

The youth, when he perceived that he had once more become his old self, put on his clothes; and now, having seen what a terrible thing, and by his own experience proved what a hideous and ugly thing Death was, he made his way back to Ostia by the shortest and the quickest way he knew without saying any more farewell words to the old woman, occupying himself for the future in reaching after Life and flying from Death, devoting himself more diligently to the consideration of those matters which he had hitherto neglected.

It now only remained that Lionora should propose her enigma, so she gave out the following one in merry wise:

> About a meadow fair and wide,
> Gay decked with flowers on every side,
> Three nymphs on task divine intent,
> Pass to and fro, and firmly bent
> To speed their work, nor night nor day
> Take pause, nor rest upon their way.
> One in her left the distaff plies,
> Between another's feet swift flies
> The spindle, and last one doth stand

With keen-edged weapon in her hand,
And cuts in twain the fragile strand.

This enigma was very easily understood by all the company, because it was clear that the fine and spacious meadow must be this world in which all men dwell. The three nymphs are the three sisters, Clotho, Lachesis, and Atropos, who by the fancy of the poets are held to represent the beginning, the middle, and the end of our lives. Clotho, who holds the rock, shows forth our birth ; Lachesis who spins it, the season of our existence, and Atropos, who severs the thread just spun by Lachesis, inevitable Death.

Already the watchful cock, bird sacred to Mercury, had given signal by his crowing of the approaching dawn, when the Signora brought to an end the storytelling for the night, and all the guests departed to their own homes, pledged, however, to return on the following evening under whatever penalty the Signora might deem fitting to inflict.

The End of the Fourth Night.

Night the Fifth.

THE sun, the glory of the smiling firmament, the measurer of our fleeting time, and the true eye of the universe, from whom likewise the horned moon and all the stars receive their radiance, had at last hidden his red and burning rays beneath the waters of the sea, and the chaste daughter of Latona, circled around by bright and beaming stars, was already lighting up the clustering shadows of the obscure night, and the shepherds, quitting the wide and open fields and the fresh herbage and the cool and limpid streams, had taken their way back with their flocks to their wonted folds, • and, worn out and weary as they were, had sunk into deep slumber on the beds of soft and yielding rushes, when the fair

and noble troop of companions, letting
go thought of everything else, hastened
to the place of meeting.   And when it
had been signified to the Signora that all
had come, and that it was now time to
recommence the story-telling, she, es-
corted in courteous and reverent wise by
the other ladies, went joyful and smiling with soft and measured step to the
hall of meeting.   Then having graciously
greeted the company of friends with glad-
some face, she ordered them to bring out
the vase of gold.   In this were put the
names of five ladies, and of these the first
to come out was that of Eritrea, the second that of Alteria, the third that of
Lauretta, the fourth that of Arianna, and
the last that of Cateruzza.   When this
was done they all began to dance to the
music of the flutes, and to pass from one
to another pleasant and loving words.
• Immediately after the end of the dance,
three damsels, by leave of the Signora,
began the following song.

SONG.

Madonna, when the springs of passion rise,
And through thy fair sweet bosom surge and
    swell;
    And in those lucent sacred eyes,
Which tell me I may live, and eke my death may
    tell;
    From those gracious looks and kind,
    A gracious hope my longings find.
    Now calm, and now spurred on by rage,
    With hope and fear a fight I wage;
    Eftsoons my hope the vantage gains,
    And I am rid of all my pains,
    And know no stroke of fate can lure,
    Or drive me from my course secure.
    Wherefore I bless the passing days;
    Great nature, and the stars I praise,
    That thy fair self my passion fired,
    Thy service sweet my song inspired.

As soon as the three damsels had
brought to an end their amorous can-
zonet, which seemed to break up the air
around into sighs of passion, the Signora
made a sign to Eritrea, who had been
chosen for the first place this evening,
that she should make a beginning of her
story-telling. The damsel, seeing that

she could in no wise excuse herself, put
aside all bashfulness, and began to speak
in turn that the order which had hitherto
prevailed might not be disturbed.

THE FIRST FABLE.

*Guerrino, only son of Filippomaria, King of
Sicily, sets free from his father's prison a
certain savage man. His mother, through
fear of the king, drives her son into exile, and
him the savage man, now humanized, delivers
from many and measureless ills.*

 HAVE heard by report, and
likewise gathered from my
own experience, most gracious
and pleasure-loving ladies, that
a kindly service done to another (although at the time the one served may
seem in no sense grateful for the boon
conferred) will more often than not
come back to the doer thereof with abundant usury of benefit. Which thing happened to the son of a king who, having
liberated from one of his father's prisons
a wild man of the woods, was more than

once rescued from a violent death by
the captive he had freed. This you will
easily understand from the fable which
I intend to relate to you, and for the
love I bear to all of you I will exhort
you never to be backward in aiding
others; because, even though you be
not repaid by those in whose behalf you
have wrought, God Himself, the re-
warder of all, will assuredly never leave
your good deed unrecompensed; nay,
on the contrary, He will make you par-
takers with Him of His divine grace.

Sicily, my dear ladies (as must be
well known to all of you), is an island
very fertile and complete in itself, and in
antiquity surpassing all the others of
which we have knowledge, abounding in
towns and villages which render it still
more beautiful. In past times the lord
of this island was a certain king named
Filippomaria, a man wise and amiable
and of rare virtue, who had to wife a
courteous, winsome, and lovely lady, the
mother of his only son, who was called

Guerrino. The king took greater delight in following the chase than any other man in the country, and, for the reason that he was of a strong and robust habit of body, this diversion was well suited to him.

Now it happened one day that, as he was coming back from hunting in company with divers of his barons and huntsmen, he saw, coming out of a thick wood a wild man, tall and big and so deformed and ugly that they all looked upon him with amazement. In strength of body he seemed no whit inferior to any of them; wherefore the king, having put himself in fighting trim, together with two of the most valiant of his barons, attacked him boldly, and after a long and doughty struggle overcame him and took him a prisoner with his own hands. Then, having bound him, they conveyed him back to the palace, and selected for him a safe lodging, fitted for the purpose, into which they cast him, and there under strong locks he was kept by the

king's command closely confined and
guarded. And seeing that the king set
high store upon his captive, he ordained
that the keys of the prison should be
held in charge by the queen, and never
a day passed when he would not for
pastime go to visit him.

Before many days had gone by the
king once more put himself in array for
the chase, and, having furnished himself
with all the various things which are
necessary thereto, he set forth with a gallant company of courtiers, but before he
left he gave into the queen's care the keys
of the prison. And during the time that
the king was absent on his hunting a great
longing came over Guerrino, who was at
that season a young lad, to see the wild
man of the woods; so having betaken
himself all alone, carrying his bow, in
which he delighted greatly, to the prison
grating, the creature saw him and straightway began to converse with him in decent
orderly fashion. And while they talked
thus, the wild man, who was caressing

the boy, dexterously snatched out of his
hand the arrow, which was richly ornamented.   Whereupon the boy began to
weep, and could not keep back his tears,
crying out that the savage ought to give
him back his arrow.   But the wild man
said to him : ' If you will open the door
and let me go free from this prison I
will give you back your arrow, but if you
refuse I will not let you have it.'   The
boy answered, ' How would you that I
should open the door for you and set
you free, seeing that I have not the means
therefor.'   Then said the wild man, ' If
indeed you were in the mood to release
me and to let me out of this narrow cell,
I would soon teach you the way in which
it might be done.'   ' But how?' replied
Guerrino ; ' tell me the way.'   To which
the wild man made answer : ' Go to the
chamber of the queen your mother, and
when you see that she is taking her mid-
day sleep, put your hand softly under
the pillow upon which she is resting, and
take therefrom the keys of the prison in

such wise that she shall not notice the
theft, and bring them here and open my
prison door.   When you shall have done
this I will give you back your arrow
forthwith, and peradventure at some
future time I may be able to make you
a return for your kindness.'

Guerrino, wishing beyond everything
to get back his gilded dart, did everything that the wild man had told him,
and found the keys exactly as he had
said, and with these in his hand he returned to the prison, and said to him :
'Behold! here are the keys; but if I let
you out of this place you must go so far
from hence that not even the scent of
you may be known, for if my father, who
is a great huntsman, should find you and
capture you again, he would of a surety
kill you out of hand.'   'Let not that
trouble you, my child,' said the captive,
'for as soon as ever you shall open the
prison and see me a free man, I will give
you back your arrow and will get me
away into such distant parts that neither

your father nor any other man shall ever find me.' Guerrino, who had all the strength of a man, worked away at the door, and finally threw open the prison, when the wild man, having given back to him his arrow and thanked him heartily, went his way.

Now this wild man had been formerly a very handsome youth, who, through despair at his inability to win the favour of the lady he ardently loved, let go all dreams of love and urbane pursuits, and took up his dwelling amongst beasts of the forest, abiding always in the gloomy woods and bosky thickets, eating grass and drinking water after the fashion of a brute. On this account the wretched man had become covered with a great fell of hair; his skin was hard, his beard thick and tangled and very long, and, through eating herbs and grass, his beard, his hairy covering, and the hair of his head had become so green that they were quite monstrous to behold.

As soon as ever the queen awoke from

her slumbers she thrust her hand under
her pillow to seek for the keys she had
put there, and, when she found they were
gone, she was terrified amain, and having turned the bed upside down without
meeting with any trace of them, she ran
straightway like one bereft of wit to the
prison, which was standing open. When
on searching further she found no sign
of the wild man, she was so sore stricken
with grief and fear that she was like to
die, and, having returned to the palace,
she made diligent search in every corner
thereof, questioning the while now this
courtier and now that as to who the presumptuous and insolent varlet was who
had been brazen enough to lay hands
upon the keys of the prison without her
knowledge. To this questioning they
one and all declared that they knew
nought of the matter which thus disturbed her. And when Guerrino met
his mother, and remarked that she was
almost beside herself in a fit of passion,
he said to her: 'Mother, see that you

your f
find n
strengt
door,
when
to him
ily, we

Nov
a very
despair
of the
dreams
took u
the for
woods
and dri
brute.
man ha
fell of h
thick an
through
his hairy
head had
quite mo
As soo

departed from the presence of his mother,
the king came back to the palace from
following the chase, and as soon as he
had alighted from his horse he betook
himself straightway to the prison to go
and see the wild man, and when he found
the door wide open and the captive
gone, and no trace of him left behind,
he was forthwith inflamed with such violent anger that he determined in his mind
to cause to be slain without fail the person who had wrought such a flagrant
misdeed. And, having sought out the
queen, who was sitting overcome with
grief in her chamber, he commanded her
to tell him what might be the name of
the impudent, rash, and presumptuous
varlet who had been bold enough of
heart to open the doors of the prison
and thereby give opportunity to the wild
man of the woods to make his escape.
Whereupon the queen, in a meek and
trembling voice, made answer to him:
O sire! be not troubled on account of
:his thing, for Guerrino our son (as he

himself has made confession to me) admits that he has done this.' And then she told to the king everything that Guerrino had said to her, and he, when he heard her story, was greatly incensed with rage. Next she told him that, on account of the fear she felt lest he should slay his son, she had sent the youth away into a far distant country, accompanied by two of their most faithful servants, and carrying with him rich store of jewels and of money sufficient to serve their needs. The king, when he listened to this speech of the queen, felt one sorrow heaping itself upon another, and he came within an ace of falling to the ground or of losing his wits, and, if it had not been for the courtiers who fell upon him and held him back, he would assuredly have slain his unhappy queen on the spot.

Now when the poor king had in some measure recovered his composure and calmed the fit of unbridled rage which had possessed him, he said to the queen:

'Alas, my wife! what fancy was this of yours which induced you to send away into some unknown land our son, the fruit of our mutual love? Is it possible that you imagined I should hold this wild man of greater value than one who was my own flesh and blood?' And without awaiting any reply to these remarks of his, he bade a great troop of soldiers mount their horses forthwith, and, after having divided themselves into four companies, to make a close search and endeavour to find the prince. But all their inquest was in vain, seeing that Guerrino and his attendants had made their journey secretly, and had let no one know who they might be.

Guerrino, after he had ridden far and traversed divers valleys and mountains and rivers, making a halt now in one spot and now in another, attained at last his sixteenth year, and so fair a youth was he by this time that he resembled nothing so much as a fresh morning rose.

But after a short time had passed, the

servants who accompanied him were
seized with the devilish thought of kill-
ing him, and then taking the store of
jewels and money and parting it amongst
themselves. This wicked plot, however,
came to nought, because by the working
of divine justice they were not able to
agree amongst themselves. For by good
fortune it happened that, one day while
they were devising this wickedness, there
rode by a very fair and graceful youth,
mounted upon a superb steed, and accou-
tred with the utmost magnificence. This
youth bowed and graciously saluted
Guerrino, and thus addressed him :
' Most gracious sir, if it should not prove
distasteful to you, I would fain make my
journey in your company.' And to this
Guerrino replied : ' Your courtesy in
making your request will not permit me
to refuse it and the pleasure of your company. Therefore I give you cordial
thanks, and I beg you as a special favour
that you will accompany us on our road.
We are strangers in this country and

know but little of its highways, and you may be able of your kindness to direct our paths therein. Moreover, as we ride on together we can discuss the various chances which have befallen us, and thus our journey will be less irksome.'

Now this young man was no other than the wild man whom Guerrino had set free from the prison of King Filippo-maria his father. This youth, after wandering through various countries and strange lands, met one day by chance a very lovely and benignant fairy, who was at that time suffering from a certain distemper. She, when she looked upon him and saw how misshapen and hideous he was, laughed so violently at the sight of his ugliness that she caused to burst an imposthume which had formed in the vicinity of her heart—an ailment which might well have caused her death by suffocation. And at that very moment she was delivered from all pain and trouble of this infirmity, as if she had never been afflicted therewith in the past, and restored to health.   Wherefore the good fairy, in recompense for so great a favour done to her, said to him, not wishing to appear ungrateful to him: 'O thou creature, who art now so deformed and filthy, since thou hast been the means of restoring to me my health which I so greatly desired, go thy ways, and be thou changed from what thou art into the fairest, the wisest, and the most graceful youth that may anywhere be found.   And, besides this, I make you the sharer with me of all the power and authority conferred upon me by nature, whereby you will be able to do and to undo whatsoever you will according to your desire.'   And having presented to him a noble horse endowed with magic powers, she gave him leave to go whithersoever he would.

Thus as Guerrino journeyed along with the young man, knowing nothing as to who he might be, but well known of him the while, they came at last to a mighty and strong city called Irlanda, over which at that time ruled King Zifroi.   This

..ifroi was the father of two daugh-
_raceful to look upon, of modest
.rs, and in beauty surpassing Venus
f, one of them named Potentiana
·he other Eleuteria. They were
.o dear by the king their father, that
·uld see by no other eyes than theirs.
.oon as Guerrino entered the city of
ıda with the unknown youth and
ı his train of servants, he hired a lodg-
of a certain householder who was the
·tiest fellow in the whole of Irlanda,
d who treated his guests with cheer of
ʰe best. And on the day following, the
·nknown youth made believe that he
·nust needs depart and travel into another
country, and went to take leave of Guerrino, thanking him in hearty wise for the
boon of his company and good usage,
but Guerrino, who had conceived the
strongest love and friendship for him,
would on no account let him go, and
showed him such strong evidence of his
good feeling that in the end the young
man agreed to tarry with him.

In the country round about Irlanda
there lived at this time two very fearful
and savage animals, one of which was a
wild horse, and the other a mare of like
nature, and so ferocious and cruel were
these beasts that they not only ravaged
and devastated all the fair cultivated
fields, but likewise killed all the animals
and the men and women dwelling therein.   And through the ruin wrought by
these beasts the country had come to
such piteous condition that no one was
found willing to abide there, so that the
peasants abandoned their farms and the
homes which were dear to them and betook themselves to find dwelling-places
in another land.   And there was nowhere
to be found any man strong and bold
enough to face them, much less to fight
with them and slay them.   Wherefore the
king, seeing that the whole country was
being made desolate of all victuals, and
of cattle, and of human creatures, and
not knowing how to devise any remedy
for this wretched pass, gave way to dolor-

ous lamentations, and cursed the hard
and evil fortune which had befallen him.
The two servants of Guerrino, who during the journey had not been able to carry
out their wicked intent through want of
concord between themselves, and on account of the arrival of the unknown
youth, now deliberated how they might
compass Guerrino's death and remain
possessors of the money and jewels, and
said one to the other: 'Let us now see
and take counsel together how we may
easiest take the life of our master.' But
not being able to find any means thereto
which seemed fitting, seeing that they
would stand in peril of losing their own
lives by the law if they should kill him,
they decided to speak privily with their
host and to tell him that Guerrino was a
youth of great prowess and valour; furthermore, that he had often boasted in
their presence that he would be ready to
slay this wild horse without incurring any
danger to himself. Thus they reasoned
with themselves: 'Now this saying may

easily come to the ears of the king, who,
being so keenly set on the destruction of
these two animals and on safeguarding
the welfare of his country, will straightway command them to bring Guerrino
before him, and will then inquire of the
youth in what manner he means to accomplish this feat.   Then Guerrino,
knowing nothing what to say or to do,
will at once be put to death by the king,
and we shall remain sole masters of the
jewels and the money.'   And they forthwith set to work to put this wicked plan
of theirs into action.

The host, when he listened to this
speech, rejoiced amain, and was as glad
as any man in all the world, and without
losing a moment of time he ran swiftly
to the palace, and having knelt down before the king and made due reverence,
he said to him secretly, 'Gracious king,
I have come to tell you that there is at
present sojourning in my hostel a fair
and gallant knight errant, who is called
by name Guerrino.   Now whilst I was

confabulating about divers matters with his servants they told me, amongst other things, how their master was a man of great prowess and well skilled in the use and practice of arms, and that in this our time one might search in vain to find another who could be compared with him. Moreover, they had many and many a time heard him boast that of his strength and valour he could without difficulty overcome and slay the wild horse which is working such dire loss and damage to your kingdom.'

When King Zifroi heard these words he immediately gave command that Guerrino should be brought before him. Whereupon the innkeeper, obedient to the word of the king, returned at once to his inn and said to Guerrino that he was to betake himself alone into the presence of the king, who greatly desired to speak with him. When Guerrino heard this he went straightway to the palace and presented himself to the king, and after saluting him with becoming reverence

begged to be told for what reason he had
been honoured with the royal commands.
To this Zifroi the king made answer:
' Guerrino, the reason which has induced
me to send for you is that I have heard
you are a knight of great valour, and one
excelling all the other knights now alive
in the world. They tell me, too, that
you have many and many a time declared
that you are strong and valorous enough
to overcome and slay the wild horse
which is working such cruel ruin and
devastation to this my kingdom, without
risk of hurt to yourself or to others. If
you can pluck up courage enough to
make trial of an emprise so full of honour as this, and prove yourself a conqueror, I promise you by this head of
mine to bestow upon you a gift which
will make you a happy man for the rest
of your days.'

Guerrino, when he heard this proposition of the king, so grave and weighty,
was mightily amazed, and at once denied
that he had ever spoken such words as

had been attributed to him. The king,
who was greatly disconcerted at this answer of Guerrino, thus addressed him :
' Guerrino, it is my will that you should
without delay undertake this task, and
be sure if you refuse and fail to comply
with my wishes I will take away your
life.' The king, having thus spoken,
dismissed from his presence Guerrino,
who returned to his inn overwhelmed
with deep sorrow, which he did not dare
to disclose to anyone. Whereupon the
unknown youth, marking that Guerrino,
contrary to his wont, was plunged in
melancholy, inquired the reason why he
was so sad and full of grief. Then Guerrino, on account of the brotherly love
subsisting between them, and finding
himself unable to refuse this just and
kind request, told him word for word
everything that had happened to him.
As soon as the unknown youth heard
this, he said, ' Be of good cheer, and put
aside all doubts and fears, for I will point
out to you a way by which you will save

your life, and be a conqueror in your enterprise, and fulfil the wishes of the king.
Return, therefore, to the king, and beg
of him to grant you the service of a skilful blacksmith.   Then order this smith
to make for you four horseshoes, which
must be thicker and broader by the
breadth of two fingers than the ordinary
measure of horseshoes, well roughed,
and each one to be fitted behind with
two spikes of a finger's length and sharp-
ened to a point.   And when these shoes
are prepared, you must have my horse,
which is enchanted, shod therewith, and
then you need have no further fear of
anything.'

Guerrino, after he had heard these
words, returned to the presence of the
king, and told him everything as the
young man had directed him.   The king
then caused to be brought before him a
well-skilled marshal smith, to whom he
gave orders that he should carry out
whatever work Guerrino might require
of him.   When they had gone to the

smith's forge, Guerrino instructed him
how to make the four horseshoes according to the words of the young stranger,
but when the smith understood in what
fashion he was required to make these
shoes, he mocked at Guerrino, and treated
him like a madman, for this way of making shoes was quite strange and unknown
to him. When Guerrino saw that the
marshal smith was inclined to mock him,
and unwilling to serve him as he had been
ordered, he went once more to the king,
and complained that the smith would
not carry out his directions. Wherefore the king bade them bring the marshal before him, and gave him express
command that, under pain of his highest displeasure, he should at once carry
out the duties which had been imposed
upon him, or, failing this, he himself
should forthwith make ready to carry
out the perilous task which had been
assigned to Guerrino. The smith, thus
hard pressed by the orders of the king,
made the horseshoes in the way described

by Guerrino, and shod the horse therewith.

When the horse was thus shod and
well-accoutred with everything that was
necessary for the enterprise, the young
stranger addressed Guerrino in these
words: 'Now mount quickly this my
horse, and go in peace, and as soon as
you shall hear the neighing of the wild
horse dismount at once, and, having
taken off from him his saddle and his
bridle, let him range at will. You yourself climb up into a high tree, and there
await the issue of the enterprise.' Guerrino, having been fully instructed by his
dear companion in all that he ought to
do, took his leave, and departed with a
light heart.

Already the glorious news had been
spread abroad through all the parts of
Irlanda how a valiant and handsome
young knight had undertaken to subju-
gate and capture the wild horse and to
present him to the king, and for this
reason everyone in the city, men and

women alike, all flew to their windows
to see him go by on his perilous errand.
When they marked how handsome and
young and gallant he was, their hearts
were moved to pity on his account, and
they said one to another, ' Ah, the poor
youth ! with what a willing spirit he goes
to his death. Of a surety it is a piteous
thing that so valiant a youth should thus
wretchedly perish.' And they could none
of them keep back their tears on account
of the compassion they felt.

But Guerrino, full of manly boldness,
went on his way blithely, and when he
had come to the spot where the wild
horse was wont to abide, and heard the
sound of his neigh, he got down from
his own horse, and having taken the
saddle and bridle therefrom he let him
go free, and himself climbed up into
the branches of a great oak, and there
awaited the fierce and bloody contest.

Scarcely had Guerrino climbed up into
the tree when the wild horse appeared
and forthwith attacked the fairy horse,

and then the two beasts engaged in the fiercest struggle that the world had ever seen, for they rushed at one another as if they had been two unchained lions, and they foamed at the mouth as if they had been bristly wild-boars pursued by savage and eager hounds.   Then, after they had fought for some time with the greatest fury, the fairy horse dealt the wild horse two kicks full on the jaw, which was put out of joint thereby; wherefore the wild horse was at once disabled, and could no longer either fight or defend himself.   When Guerrino saw this he rejoiced greatly, and having come down from the oak, he took a halter which he had brought with him and secured the wild horse therewith, and led him with his dislocated jaw back to the city, where he was welcomed by all the people with the greatest joy.   According to his promise he presented the horse to the king, who, together with all the inhabitants of the city, held high festival, and rejoiced amain over the gallant deed wrought by Guerrino.

But the servants of Guerrino were
greatly overcome with grief and confusion, inasmuch as their evil designs had
miscarried; wherefore, inflamed with rage
and hatred, they once more let it come
to the hearing of King Zifroi that Guerrino had vaunted that he could with the
greatest ease kill the wild mare also whenever it might please him. When the
king heard this he laid exactly the same
commands on Guerrino as he had done
in the matter of the horse, and because
the youth refused to undertake this task,
which appeared to him impossible, the
king threatened to have him hung up by
one foot as a rebel against his crown.
After Guerrino had returned to his inn,
he told everything to his unknown companion, who smilingly said : ' My good
brother, fret not yourself because of this,
but go and find the marshal smith, and
command him to make for you four more
horseshoes, as big again as the last, and
see that they are duly furnished with good
sharp spikes. Then you must follow

exactly the same course as you took with
the horse, and you will return here
covered with greater honour than ever.'
When therefore he had commanded to
be made the sharply-spiked horseshoes,
and had caused the valiant fairy horse to
be shod therewith, he set forth on his
gallant enterprise.

As soon as Guerrino had come to the
spot where the wild mare was wont to
graze, and heard her neighing, he did
everything exactly in the same manner
as before, and when he had set free the
fairy horse, the mare came towards it and
attacked it with such fierce and terrible
biting that it could with difficulty defend
itself against such an attack.   But it bore
the assault valiantly, and at last succeeded
in planting so sharp and dexterous a kick
on the mare that she was lamed in her
right leg, whereupon Guerrino came
down from the high tree into which he
had climbed, and having captured her,
bound her securely.   Then he mounted
his own horse and rode back to the pal-

ace, where he presented the wild mare
to the king, amidst the rejoicings and
acclamations of all the people. And
everyone, attracted by wonderment and
curiosity, ran to see this wild beast,
which, on account of the grave injuries
she had received in the fight, soon died.
And by these means the country was
freed from the great plague which had
for so long a time vexed it.

Now when Guerrino had returned to
his hostel, and had betaken himself to
repose somewhat on account of the weariness which had come over him, he found
that he was unable to get any sleep by
reason of a strange noise which he heard
somewhere in the chamber. Wherefore,
having risen from his couch, he perceived
that there was something, I know not
what, beating about inside a pot of honey,
and not able to get out. So Guerrino
opened the honey-pot, and saw within
a large hornet, which was struggling with
its wings without being able to free itself
from the honey around it. Moved by

pity, he took hold of the insect and let
it go free.

Now Zifroi the king had as yet given
to Guerrino no reward for the two valiant deeds which he had wrought, but he
was conscious in his heart that he would
be acting in a very base fashion were he
to leave such great valour without a rich
guerdon, so he caused Guerrino to be
called into his presence, and thus addressed him : ' Guerrino, by your noble
deeds the whole of my kingdom is now
free from the scourge, therefore I intend
to reward you for the great benefits you
have wrought in our behalf; but as I
can conceive of no other gift which would
be worthy and sufficient for your merits,
I have determined to give you one of
my two daughters to wife. But you
must know that of these two sisters one
is called Potentiana, and she has hair
braided in such marvellous wise that it
shines like golden coils. The other is
called Eleuteria, and her tresses are of
such texture that they flash brightly like

the finest silver. Now if you can guess
—the maidens being closely veiled the
while—which is she of the golden tresses,
I will give her to you as your wife, together with a mighty dowry of money ;
but if you fail in this, I will have your
head struck off your shoulders.'

Guerrino, when he heard this cruel
ordeal which was proposed by Zifroi the
king, was mightily amazed, and turning
to him spake thus : ' O gracious sovereign ! Is this a worthy guerdon for all
the perils and fatigues I have undergone?
Is this a reward for the strength I have
spent on your behalf? Is this the gratitude you give me for having delivered
your country from the scourge by which
it was of late laid desolate? Alas ! I
did not merit this return, which of a
truth is not a deed worthy of such a
mighty king as yourself. But since this
is your pleasure and I am helpless in
your hands, you must do with me what
pleases you best.' ' Now go,' said Zifroi,
'and tarry no longer in my presence.

the time come when I shall be able to
make you some repayment for all the
kind offices you have done me? Certes,
were I to live for a thousand years, I
should never have it in my power to
recompense you the very smallest portion
thereof. But that one, who is the re-
warder of all, will in this matter make
up for me in that respect in which I am
wanting.' To this speech of Guerrino
his companion made answer: 'Guerrino,
my brother, there is in sooth no need
for you to trouble yourself about making
any return to me for the services I may
have wrought you, but assuredly it is
now full time that I should reveal to you,
and that you should know clearly who I
am. For in the same fashion as you
delivered me from death, I on my part
have desired to render to you the recompense you deserve so highly at my hands.
Know, then, that I am the wild man of
the woods whom you, with such loving
compassion, set free from the prison-
house of the king your father, and that

i

i
n
is
Gu

But Guerrino stood still in a state of doubt and hesitation, and answered nothing, but the king, who was mightily curious to see how the matter would end, pressed him amain to speak, crying out that time was flying, and that it behoved him to give his answer at once. To this Guerrino made answer: 'Most sacred majesty, time forsooth may be flying, but the end is not yet come to this day, which is the limit you have given me for my decision.' And all those standing by affirmed that Guerrino only claimed his right.

When, therefore, the king and Guerrino and all the others had stood for a long time in expectation, behold! there suddenly appeared a hornet, which at once began to fly and buzz round the head and the fair face of Potentiana of the golden hair. And she, as if she were afeared of the thing, raised her hand to drive it away, and when she had done this three times the hornet flew away out of sight. But even after this sign Guerrino remained uncertain for a short time, although he had full faith in the words of Rubinetto, his well-beloved companion. Then said the king, 'How now, Guerrino, what do you say? The time has now come when you must put an end to this delay, and make up your mind.' And Guerrino, having looked well first at one and then at the other of the maidens, put his hand on the head of Potentiana, who had been pointed out to him by the hornet, and said, 'Gracious king, this one is your daughter of the golden tresses.' And when the maiden had raised her veil it was clearly proved that it was indeed she, greatly to the joy of all those who were present, and to the satisfaction of the people of the city. And Zifroi the king gave her to Guerrino as his wife, and they did not depart thence until Rubinetto had wedded the other sister. After this Guerrino declared himself to be the son of Filippomaria, King of Sicily, hearing which Zifroi was greatly rejoiced, and caused the marriages

Guerrino And Polentiana Of The Golden Tresses

Night the Fifth

FIRST FABLE

Guerrino And Polentiana Of The Golden Tresses

Night the Fifth

FIRST FABLE

Guarino And Polentana Of The
Golden Tresses

to be celebrated with the greatest pomp and magnificence.

When this news came to the father and the mother of Guerrino they felt the greatest joy and contentment, seeing that they had by this time given up their son as lost. When he returned to Sicily with his dear wife and his well-loved brother and sister-in-law, they all received a gracious and loving welcome from his father and mother, and they lived a long time in peace and happiness, and he left behind him fair children as the heirs of his kingdom.

This touching story told by Eritrea won the highest praise of all the hearers, and she, when she saw that all were silent, proposed her enigma in the following words:

A cruel beast of nature dread
From out a tiny germ is bred.
In hate all beings else it holds,
And each one trembles who beholds
Its form of fear. Death all around
It spreads, and oft itself is found
The victim of its fatal rage,
And war on all the world will wage.

Beneath its breath the trees decay,
The living plants will fade away.
A beast more cruel, fierce, and fell,
Ne'er rose from out the pit of hell.

When the enigma set to the worshipful company by the clever damsel had
been considered and highly praised by
everyone, some found one solution therefor and some another, but not one of
them gave the one which rightly ex-
plained its meaning. Wherefore Eritrea,
seeing that her riddle had not been understood, said, " It seems to me that the
cruel animal I have described cannot be
anything else than the basilisk, which
hates all other living beasts in the world,
and slays them with its sharp and pier-
cing glances. And if peradventure it
should chance to see its own form mir-
rored anywhere, it straightway dies."
When Eritrea had come to the end of
the interpretation of her enigma, the
Signor Evangelist,[1] who sat by her side,
said to her smiling: " Of a truth you

[1] Pietro Bembo.

yourself are this basilisk, signora, for with your beautiful eyes you bring soft death to all those who gaze upon you." But Eritrea, with her cheeks suffused with the lovely tint of nature, answered nought. Alteria sat near by, and, as soon as she perceived that the enigma was now completed, having been highly praised by all, she called to mind that it was now her turn to tell a story according to the Signora's pleasure, so she began in the following wise a fable which proved in the end to be fully as mirthful as it was commendable.

THE SECOND FABLE.

Adamantina, the daughter of Bagolana Sabonese, by the working of a certain doll becomes the wife of Drusiano, King of Bohemia.

O powerful, so commanding, so subtle is the wit of man that without doubt it may be held to overtop and to exceed every other human force to be found in the world; wherefore it has been said, not without just cause, that the wise man is the governor of the stars. This saying recalls to my memory a fable, by the telling of which I hope to make quite clear to you how a young girl, of mean estate and very poor, was succoured by fortune, and in the end became the wife of a mighty king. Although my fable will be very short, it may, if I mistake not, be found to be none the less pleasing and diverting on that account. I beg you therefore to lend me your ears attentively, and listen to me, as hitherto you have listened to our very worthy associates, who, of a surety, have merited from you praise rather than blame.

In the country of Bohemia, dear ladies, there lived not a long time ago a little old woman known by the name of Bagolana Savonese, miserably poor in her way of life, and the mother of two daughters, one of whom was called Cassandra and the other Adamantina. Now this woman, though she had scarce any-

thing to call her own, was anxious to
set her affairs in order, so that she might
die in peace, and as the whole of the
wealth that she had to dispose of in her
house and out of it consisted of a small
coffer filled with tow, she made her will
and gave this coffer and what it contained
to her two daughters, begging them at
the same time to live peacefully together
after she should be dead.

These two sisters, though they were
very poor in any of the endowments of
fortune, were by no means wanting in
mental gifts, so that in all virtues and in
righteous behaviour they were no whit
inferior to other women. After the old
woman was dead and her body had been
buried, Cassandra, who was the elder
sister of the two, took a pound of the
tow and sat down and began to spin the
same with great care, and, as soon as she
had spun it, she gave the thread she had
made to Adamantina, her younger sister,
bidding her to take it out into the piazza
and to sell it, and with the proceeds of

the sale to purchase some bread wherewith they might keep themselves alive.
Thereupon Adamantina took the thread,
and, having put it under her arm, she
went her way into the piazza to sell her
wares, according to the commandment
of her sister Cassandra; but, as chance
would have it, what she did ran entirely
counter to her own wishes and to those
of her sister, for as she was walking in
the piazza she happened to meet there
an old woman who was carrying in her
apron the most beautiful and most perfectly made doll that had ever been
seen. So much indeed was Adamantina's fancy taken by the doll that, after
she had looked at it and feasted her eyes
upon it, her thoughts were more occupied in considering how she might
become the owner thereof, than how she
should dispose of her yarn.   Therefore
Adamantina, letting her thoughts run on
in this wise, and not knowing how to
get possession of the doll by anything
she might say or do, made up her mind

at last to tempt fortune and to see
whether she could not obtain the doll
through exchange. So having gone up
to the old woman she spake thus: 'Good
mother, if it seem a fair thing to you,
I will gladly give you this thread of
mine in barter for your doll.' The old
woman, when she saw that this fine
handsome young girl was so eager to
have the doll for her own, was not disposed to baulk her fancy; so, having
taken the thread, she handed the doll
over to Adamantina.

As soon as the girl could call the doll
her own, she went back to her home as
joyous and content as anyone in all the
world, and her sister Cassandra, when she
saw her, at once inquired of her whether
she had sold the yarn. To this Adamantina replied that she had sold it. 'But
where is the bread which you have bought
with the price you got for the thread?'
inquired Cassandra. Then Adamantina
opened wide the apron she was wearing
and showed Cassandra the doll which

she had got by barter of her own ware.
Cassandra, who was sorely hungry and
eager for the bread, when she saw the
doll was filled with such violent anger
and indignation that she seized Adamantina by the hair of her head, and
belaboured her so grievously with cuffs
and blows that the unfortunate girl could
scarcely move. Adamantina took the
blows with patience, and, without making any attempt to defend herself, she
went away and hid herself in another
room, taking her doll with her.

When the evening had come Adamantina, according to the habit of young
girls, sat down by the fireside, and, having taken some oil out of the lamp, she
anointed therewith the doll's stomach
and loins. Then she wrapped the doll
carefully in some bits of tattered cloth,
and placed it in her own bed, and a very
short time afterwards she went to bed
herself and lay down beside the doll.
Scarcely had Adamantina fallen into her
first sleep when the doll began to cry

out: ' The stool, mother, the stool.'
Whereupon Adamantina, wakening from
her sleep, said : ' What is the matter with
you, my daughter?' and to this the doll
replied in the same words as before.
Then Adamantina said : ' Wait a little,
my daughter ; ' and she straightway arose
and ministered to the doll as if it had
been a young child, and to her amazement she found that the doll filled the
stool with a great quantity of coins of
all sorts.

As soon as Adamantina saw what had
happened she straightway awakened her
sister Cassandra and showed her the
money which had come to her in this
strange fashion. Cassandra, when she
marked what a great sum of money was
there, stood as one stricken with wonder,
and rendered hearty thanks to God for
sending them such welcome succour in
their want and misery, and, turning to
Adamantina, she begged pardon of her
for the blows which she had so cruelly
and unjustly given to her, and she took

the doll and caressed it tenderly and kissed it, holding it closely in her arms. And when the next day had come, the two sisters took of the money and purchased therewith bread and wine and oil and wood, and all other sorts of provisions which are suitable to a well-ordered house, taking care every evening to anoint the stomach of the doll with oil, and to wrap it in a piece of the finest linen, and the doll on its part never failed to supply them with money in abundance whenever they had need thereof.

It chanced on a certain day that one of their neighbours, having gone into the house of the two sisters, remarked that their home was well furnished with all the necessaries of life in great abundance, and on this account began to wonder how it was that they could have become rich in so short a time, remembering, moreover, how miserably poor they had been hitherto, and knowing full well that no one could say otherwise than that they were honest and upright in all their

ways. Wherefore the neighbour, having
given the matter due consideration, determined to find out the source from
which they might have gathered such
gain; so having betaken herself once
more to the house of the two sisters, she
thus addressed them: 'My daughters,
I beg you to tell me by what means you
have been able to furnish your house so
plentifully, seeing that but yesterday you
were in sore poverty.'   To this question
Cassandra, the elder sister, made reply:
'Good neighbour, we have done all this
by the means of a single pound of flaxen
yarn, which we gave in exchange for a
doll, and this doll gives us money in
abundance, and supplies us with everything we need.'   The neighbour, when
she heard these words was greatly disturbed in her mind, and was so filled
with envy of the good fortune which had
befallen the girls that she determined to
steal the doll.   As soon as she returned
to her house, she told her husband how
the two sisters had a certain doll which

every night was accustomed to give them great store of gold and silver, and that she had made up her mind to steal the doll from them come what might.

Now although the husband made mock of his wife's words at first, she went on telling her story with such a show of reason that in the end she convinced him that it was nought but the truth.   But he said to his wife: 'And how do you mean to steal it?'   To this the good woman made answer: 'To-night you must feign to be drunk, and, having caught up your sword, you must run after me threatening to take my life, but at the same time only striking the wall.   And I, pretending to be in great terror of you, will run out of the house into the street, and the two sisters, who are kindly and compassionate by nature, will assuredly open their door to me, and take me in and shelter me. I will stay there for the night, and will do the best I can for the futherance of my plan.'

And when the evening had come, the

husband of this good dame took a rusty
old sword of his, and, laying about with
it now against this wall and now against
that, ran after his wife, who, screaming
and crying with a loud voice, fled out of
the house. The two sisters, when they
heard this hurlyburly, ran to look out
into the street to see what might be the
cause thereof, whereupon they recognized the voice of their neighbour, who
was screaming lustily. They at once
rushed away from the window, and ran
down to the door giving on to the street,
and having opened this they pulled her
into the house. The good woman, when
she had been questioned by them for
what reason her husband had pursued
and assaulted her with such anger, thus
made reply: 'This evening he came home
so dazed with winebibbing that he wots
not anything that he does. And only
for the reason that I reproved him on account of his drunkenness, he seized his
sword and ran after me threatening to kill
me; but as I am more nimble and swift

every night was accustomed to give
them great store of gold and silver, and
that she had made up her mind to steal
the doll from them come what might.

Now although the husband made much
of his wife's words at first, she went on
telling her story with such a show of
reason that in the end she convinced him
that it was nought but the truth. But he
said to his wife: 'And how do you make good
to steal it?' To this the good woman
made answer: 'To-night you must feign
to be drunk, and, having caught up your
sword, you must run after me threatening
to take my life, but at the same time
striking the wall. And I, pretending to
be in great terror of you, will run out of
the house into the street, and the
ters, who are kindly and compassionate
by nature, will assuredly open their
to me, and take me in and shelter me. This
I will stay there for the night, and
do the best I can for the further
my plan.'

And when the evening had

⸱⸱ty of money that the doll
the two sisters. However,
⸱⸱e was mightily anxious to
⸱ experiment on the follow-
⸱⸱ husband, who was in no
⸱⸱ce again the discomfort he
⸱⸱, began to abuse her round-
⸱⸱ched against her the most
⸱ speeches that ever man ap-
⸱⸱an. Not content with this,
⸱⸱e doll in his hand, and hav-
⸱ the window, he hurled it
⸱⸱ street, letting it fall upon a
⸱⸱epings which lay below. Soon
⸱⸱ done this, it happened that
⸱⸱ants who tilled the ground
⸱ city loaded on their cart this
⸱⸱se, and without knowing what
⸱⸱ded up the doll likewise, and
had filled their cart they re-
the country, and spread the
⸱⸱eepings over their fields in
⸱⸱rich the soil.
⸱ny days after this, it chanced
⸱⸱no the king, who had gone

out into the country to seek diversion
in the chase, was seized with a sharp pain
of his intestines, and forthwith sought
relief of the same by the remedy of nature, but not having upon him wherewith to accommodate himself afterwards,
he called to him one of his servants and
charged him to go search for something
which might serve his ends. Whereupon the servant went towards the ma-
nure heap which the peasants aforesaid
had collected, to see whether he might
be able to find anything which would be
suitable for the purpose, and, looking
now on this side and now on that, his
eye fell upon the doll, and having picked
it up, he bore it at once to the king, who
without any fear or suspicion, took hold
of it and proceeded to apply it to the
use for which he wanted it. But the
next moment the king broke out into
loud cries and bellowings of pain, for the
doll had seized upon his hinder parts
with its teeth, and held on thereto with
so tight a grip that he screamed out with

agony at the top of his voice. And
when those of his train heard these terrible cries, they forthwith all ran towards
the king to lend him their aid. Seeing
him lying on the ground more dead than
alive, they were hugely astonished to
find that he was suffering pain on account of the doll which had fastened on
to him, and they began at once with
their united strength to try to disengage
it from his hinder parts; but all their
strivings were in vain, for the more violently they tugged to get the thing away,
the greater torment it inflicted on the
poor king, and there was not one of them
who could disturb its hold, much less
make it let go. And now and again the
doll would claw him with its sharp fingers so grievously that he seemed to see
all the stars of the firmament, although
it was yet high noon.

When the unfortunate king had returned to his palace with the doll still
hanging on to him, and was still unable
to find any means of getting rid of his

plague, he caused to be put forth a proclamation declaring that any man, no
matter what his condition might be, who
should have the wit and courage to re-
move the doll should be rewarded by a
gift of one third part of the king's do-
minions, and if it should chance that
any maiden might be found able to perform this work he would take her for
his beloved wife.   And in addition to
this King Drusiano swore by his crown,
and bound himself by the most solemn
oaths to keep every promise he had made
in the proclamation above named.   As
soon as the king's proclamation was
made public, a vast crowd of people repaired to the palace in the hope of ob-
taining the promised reward, but to not
one of them was granted the good fortune of being able to rid the king of his
trouble; on the contrary, as soon as anyone chanced to come near the king the
doll tormented him more grievously than
ever, so the wretched Drusiano, thus
cruelly vexed and tortured, and unable

to light upon any remedy for his strange
and incomprehensible affliction, lay there
almost as if he were a dead man.

Cassandra and Adamantina, who in
the meantime had shed many tears over
the loss of their doll, as soon as they
heard the terms of the proclamation
which had been issued, went straightway
to the palace and presented themselves
before the king. Then Cassandra, who
was the elder of the two, began at once
to fondle and caress the doll with signs
of the greatest affection, but thereupon,
so far from loosening its hold, it only
vexed the poor king yet more sorely with
its teeth and claws. Then Adamantina,
who stood somewhat apart from the
others, now came forward and said: 'Gracious king! I beg you that you will now
suffer me to try my fortune in ridding
you of this ill,' and, having gone close
to the doll, she spake thus: 'Ah, my
child! leave my lord the king in peace
now, and do not torment him any longer.'
And with these words she took hold of

it by its clothes, and began to fondle and caress it. The doll, as soon as it recognized its own little mother, who had been in the habit of tending and caring for it, at once let go its hold on the king's person and sprang into Adamantina's arms. And when Drusiano perceived what was done, he was utterly astonished and amazed, and forthwith lay down to get some repose, for during many and many nights and days he had not been able to find either rest or peace on account of the sharp agony he had undergone.

When King Drusiano was at length healed of the ills that had befallen him on account of the biting of the doll, in order that he might not fail in the fulfilment of the promise he had made, he caused Adamantina to be brought into his presence, and, seeing that she was a fair and graceful young maiden, he married her in the presence of all his people. A short time afterwards he honourably bestowed her elder sister Cassandra in marriage with sumptuous feast-ings and triumphs, and they all lived long together in peace and happiness.

The doll, when it saw how both of the sisters had been so honourably and richly married, and how everything had come to a happy issue, suddenly disappeared, and whither it went and what became of it no man ever knew. But in my opinion it merely disappeared after the common fashion of phantoms.

The fable told by Alteria, which here came to an end, gave great pleasure to all the company, and the laughter was loud and long as they recalled to mind the beneficent ways and habits of the doll, and in what fashion the thing hung with its teeth and its claws upon the hinder parts of the king. And when the laughter had somewhat abated, the Signora at once gave the word to Alteria to follow the customary rule and propound her enigma, which the damsel gave in the following words, smiling pleasantly the while:

> Just a span in length is he,
> And plump in form in due degree.

Full of eagerness and pride,
And ready aye with men to bide.
Very fair his seeming shows ;
Capote red he wears and hose ;
Bells also,   A thing of pleasure
To those who love him in due measure.

As soon as Alteria had spoken the
last word of her gracefully turned and
difficult enigma, the Signora, who by
this time had put off her kindly mood
and was casting angry looks upon the
damsel, cried out that it was most unseemly to speak such immodest words
to the ears of honest women in her presence, and that for the future she must be
careful not to trespass in like manner.
Whereupon Alteria, blushing somewhat,
rose from her seat, and having turned
her bright face towards the Signora, spake
thus : " Signora, of a truth the enigma
which I have just proposed is not in any
way immodest as you seem to believe,
and this I shall make quite clear to you
by giving you the real interpretation
thereof, which I will straightway make

known to you and to the rest of my gracious hearers. For be it understood my
enigma signifies nothing else except the
falcon, which is a bird at once tractable
and bold, and comes readily to the fal-
coner's call. It wears on its feet jesses
and bells, and it will give great pleasure
and diversion to anyone who goes out
fowling therewith." When the real interpretation of this clever riddle, which
had been set down by the Signora as
being unseemly, had been given, all the
listeners praised it heartily, and the Signora, having by this time laid aside every
sinister imagining she had harboured concerning Alteria's riddle, turned her face
towards Lauretta and made a sign to her
that she should approach her, and the
damsel at once came in obedience to the
command. And because Lauretta stood
next in turn to follow with her fable, the
Signora thus addressed her : " It is my
wish that you refrain for a while from
telling us your story, and that you should
instead listen to that which the others

may say.   It is not because I hold you
in light esteem that I speak thus to you,
or rate your powers less than those of
your companions, but in order that we
may be entertained this evening in a
fashion that is beyond our wónt."   To
this Lauretta made reply : " Signora, any
word of yours is to me as a command,"
and having made a profound obeisance
to the Signora she went back to her
place.

Then the Signora, turning an earnest
gaze upon Molino's face, made a sign to
him thus with her hand to bid him come
to her, whereupon he got up quickly
from his seat and went most respectfully
towards her.   To him she spake in these
words : " Signor Antonio, this last evening of the week is for us a special time,
a season of privilege for anyone to say
whatsoever he may wish to say, so for
my own pleasure and for the pleasure of
this honourable company, I would that
you yourself should relate to us a fable
in your best and happiest vein and man-

ner, and I further beg you that you will
tell us this story in the speech of Bergamo. And if — as I hope you will —
you grant us this favour, we shall all of us
be held by a lasting obligation to you."
Molino, when he rightly understood the
Signora's speech, stood at first as one
confounded, but when he realized that
he had sailed up to a point he could not
weather, he said : " Signora, it is for you
to command and for us to obey, but I
would warn you not to expect from me
aught that shall give you any great pleasure, seeing that the illustrious damsels I
see around me have brought the art of
story-telling to such a high pitch of excellence that there is little or no chance
for one like me to contribute aught to
our diversion. Nevertheless, such as I
am, I will do my best to give you satisfaction, not, indeed, so great as you wish,
or as I would, but according to the measure of my humble powers." And having
thus spoken, Molino went-back to his seat
and began his story in the following words.

THE THIRD FABLE.

Bertholdo of Valsabbia has three sons, all of them hunchbacks and much alike in seeming. One of them, called Zambo, goes out into the world to seek his fortune, and arrives at Rome, where he is killed and thrown into the Tiber, together with his two brothers.[1]

IT is indeed hard, sweet ladies and gracious Signora! hard, indeed, I say it is, to kick against the pricks, for the kick of an ass is a cruel thing; but still more cruel is the kick of a horse, and for this reason, since fortune has willed it that I should undertake to tell a tale, I had best obey; for patience beatifies us, but obstinacy damns us, and, should we prove obstinate, we go straight to tne devil. So if it should chance that I tell you 'something which may prove in no wise to your taste, do not give the blame to me, but to the Signora over yonder who has thus willed it.

[1] Told in the dialect of Bergamo.

It often happens that a man goes a-
seeking that which he had better leave
alone, and in consequence not seldom
lights upon certain things which he never
looked to find, and in the end will be
left with his hand full of flies.[1]   Thus,
indeed, it happened some time ago to
Zambo, the son of Bertholdo of Valsabbia, who sought to dupe two of his
brothers, but by his brothers was himself duped.

True it is that in the end they all
three died miserably, as you will hear
if you will lend me your ears, and with
your minds and your understandings
listen to the story which I am now about
to relate.

I must tell you, therefore, that Bertholdo of Valsabbia, in the province of
Bergamo, had three sons, all three hunchbacks, and all resembling each other so
closely that it was impossible to tell the
one from the other; they might, indeed,
have been likened to three shrivelled

[1] Orig., *e ixi romd co li ma pieni de moschi.*

pumpkins.[1]   One of these sons was called
Zambo, another Bertaz, and the third
Santì; and Zambo, who was the eldest,
had not yet attained his sixteenth year.
It came one day to Zambo's ears that
Bertoldo his father, by reason of the
great dearth there was in the parts round
about and in all the rest of the land besides, wished to sell for the sake of his
family the small property which was his
patrimony (in sooth, there were few or
none to be found in that country who
had any belongings of their own); wherefore Zambo, addressing himself to Bertaz
and Santì, his younger brothers, spoke
to them as an elder brother in the following words: ' It would surely be a wiser
plan, my dear brothers, that our father
should retain the little bit of property
which we happen to have, so that after
his death we may have something whereby to gain a sustenance, and that you
should go out into the world and try to
earn something upon which we may keep

[1] Orig., *con sarevef à di tre penduletti sgonfi de dre.*

up our house. I, in the meantime, will remain at home with the old man, taking good care of him, and thus we shall have no need to waste our substance, and by such management may be able to tide over the season of scarcity.'

Bertaz and Santì the younger brothers, who were no less crafty and cunning than Zambo, at once made answer to their brother: 'Zambo, dear brother that you are, you spring a surprise upon us somewhat suddenly, and question us in such wise that we scarcely know how to answer you. Give us thinking time for this one night; then we will consider the matter, and to-morrow will let you have our reply.'

The two brothers, Bertaz and Santì, had been brought forth at one birth, and between these two there was a greater sympathy than between either of them and Zambo. And if Zambo were to be reckoned a rascal of twenty-two carats, Bertaz and Santì were rascals of twenty-six; for it not seldom happens that, where nature fails, ingenuity and malice supply the want.

When the following morning had come, Bertaz, by agreement with Santì his brother, went to find Zambo, and opened discourse with him in these words : 'Zambo, my dear brother, we have well thought over and considered the case in which we stand, and, seeing that you are (as you will not deny) the elder brother, we think it would be more seemly for you to go first into the world, and that we who are younger should stop here to look after our father. And we would counsel you that if, in the meantime, you should come across any good fortune for yourself and for us, you should write to us here, and we would come at once to join you.' Zambo, who had hoped to get the better of Bertaz and Santì, was greatly disconcerted when he heard this answer, and, muttering to himself, he said : 'These two are more cunning and malicious loons than I had imagined.' For he had hoped to be rid

of his two brothers, and himself be left
master of all their property, trusting that
they might both of them die of hunger
by reason of the dearth prevailing in the
land; moreover, their father was not long
for this world, and had already one foot
in the grave. But the issue of this affair
proved to be vastly different than anything Zambo had expected. When,
therefore, Zambo heard the answer given
to him by Bertaz and Santì, he made a
small bundle of the few rags he possessed, and, having filled a pouch with
some bread and cheese and a small flask·
of wine, he put on his feet a pair of shoes
of red pigskin, and departed thence and
went towards Brescia. But not finding
anything to suit him there, he went on
to Verona, where he came across a master cap-maker, who asked him whether
he knew how to make caps, to which
question he answered no; and, seeing
that there was nothing for him to do
there, he left Verona, and, having passed
through Vicenza, he came to Padua,

where certain doctors saw him and asked
him whether he knew how to take care
of mules, and he answered them no, but
that he could till the land and tend vines;
but, as he could not come to any under-
standing with them, he went on his way
to Venice.

Zambo had wandered about the city
for a long time without lighting on any
employ to his taste, and, seeing that he
had about him neither a coin, nor anything to eat, he felt that he was indeed
in evil case.   But after he had walked a
long distance, he was brought by God's
pleasure to the port, but because he
was penniless no one would assist him.
Wherefore the poor fellow knew not
which way he should turn, but having
remarked that the ragged wastrels who
turned the machines for drawing boats
ashore gained a few pence by this labour,
he took up this calling himself.   But
Fortune, who always persecutes the poor,
the slothful, and the wretched, willed that
one day when he was working one of

these machines the leather strap should
break. This in untwining caught a
spar, which hit him in the chest and
felled him to the ground, where for a
time he lay as one lifeless. Indeed, had
it not been for the timely aid given to
him by some kind-hearted fellows, who
haled him into their boat by his legs and
arms and rowed him back to Venice, he
assuredly would have died.

When Zambo had recovered from the
ill effects of this mischance he went in
search of someone who might give him
employment, and as he passed by a
grocer's shop he was remarked by the
master thereof, who was pounding in a
mortar almonds wherewith to make mar-
zapan. Whereupon the grocer asked
him whether he was minded to come
and serve in the shop, and Zambo replied that he was; so, having entered,
he was at once set to work by the grocer at dressing certain comfits, and instructed how to separate the black from
the white, working the while beside an-

other apprentice. This fellow and Zambo (greedy gluttons, forsooth), in the course of their task of comfit dressing, set to work in such a manner that they stripped off and used the outer rind of the sweet almonds and ate the kernels themselves. The grocer, when he saw what was going on, took a stick in his hand and gave each of them a sound beating, saying; ' If you are set on plunder, you thievish knaves, I would that you pilfered your own stores and not mine,' and having thus spoken he belaboured them still more and bade them go to the devil.

Zambo, smarting from the blows dealt him by the grocer, took his departure and went to St. Mark's Place, and as he passed by the spot where herbs and vegetables are set out for sale, he met by good luck a herbalist from Chiozza, Vivia Vianel by name, who straightway demanded of him whether he would be willing to enter his service, where he would get good food and good treat-

ment as well.   Zambo, who at this time
wore the armorial bearings of Siena[1] on
his back, and was longing for a good
meal, replied that he was ; so, when
Vianel had sold his few last bunches of
herbs, they took a boat and returned to
Chiozza, where Zambo was at once set
to work in the garden and bidden to
tend the vines.

Now Zambo, after he had gone up
and down in Chiozza for a certain time,
became acquainted with divers of his
master's friends, and when the season for
the first ripe figs had come, Vivia took
the three finest he could pluck from his
garden, and, having put them on a plat-
ter, sent them as a present to a friend of
his in Chiozza whose name was Peder.
He called Zambo and gave him the
three figs, and said to him : 'Zambo,
take these three figs and carry them to
my friend Ser Peder, and ask him to
accept them for love of me.'   Zambo in
obedience to Vivia's command replied :

---

[1] *i.e.*, a famished wolf.

'With pleasure, my master,' and taking the figs he merrily went his way. But it chanced by ill luck that as Zambo was going along the street a greedy humour took possession of him, and having looked at the figs over and over again he thus addressed gluttony: 'What shall I do? shall I eat or shall I refrain?' To this gluttony replied: 'A starving man observes no law; wherefore eat.' And for the reason that Zambo was greedy by nature and very hungry to boot, he listened to these counsels of gluttony, and having taken in his hands one of the figs, he began to rend the skin from the neck thereof. Then he took a bite here and a bite there, saying the while, 'It is good; it is not good;' and so he went on till he had consumed it all in tasting, and nought but the skin remained.

When Zambo had eaten the fig he began to wonder whether, perchance, he might not have transgressed somewhat, but for the reason that gluttony still

urged him on, he did not stand long in
balancing chances, but took the second
fig in his hand and treated it as he had
treated the first. After the greedy fellow had made an end of the second fig
he was again assailed by fears, and hardly
knew whether, on account of his fault,
he should go on or turn back; but after
a short term of indecision he took courage and determined to go on. As soon
as he had come to Ser Peder's door he
knocked thereat, and as he was well
known there the door was quickly
opened. Having entered he went to
find Ser Peder, who was walking up and
down, and when he saw him the good
man thus addressed him: 'What has
Zambo come to tell me? What good
news does he bring?' 'Good morrow,
good morrow,' answered Zambo; 'my
master gave me three figs to bring to
you, but of these three I have eaten
two.' 'But how could you do such a
thing as this?' said Ser Peder. 'I did
it in this fashion,' said Zambo, and with

these words he took the last fig and ate it deliberately, and so it fell out that all three of the figs found their way into Zambo's belly. When Ser Peder saw this saucy jest he said to Zambo : ' My son, tell your master that I thank him, but that in future he need not trouble himself to send me presents of this sort.' Zambo answered, ' No, no, Messer Peder, say not so, for I shall never weary of such errands,' and with these words he left Messer Peder and went home.

When the report of Zambo's smart trick came to Vivia's ears, and when he learned furthermore how finely lazy he was and a glutton as well, guzzling when he was hungry till he was ready to burst, and how he would never work save when he was driven thereto, the good man chased the hunchback out of his house. So Zambo, poor devil, when he found himself driven out of his employ, knew not whither to turn ; thus after a little he determined to go to Rome in the

hope that he might there find better fortune than he had hitherto come across,
and this plan of his he duly carried out.

Zambo, when he had arrived in Rome,
went about seeking here and there a
master, and at last met a certain merchant who was called Messer Ambros
dal Mul, who kept a great shop full of
cloth goods. With him Zambo took
service, and was set to mind the shop,
and seeing that he had suffered much in
the past, he made up his mind to learn
the trade and to live a decent life for the
future. Though he was deformed and
ugly, he was nevertheless very shrewd,
and in a short time he made himself so
useful in the shop that his master seemed
to take no more trouble himself about
buying or selling, but trusted everything
to him and made use of him for service
of all kinds. Now it chanced that one
day Messer Ambros had occasion to go
to the fair of Recanati with a stock of
cloth, but perceiving that Zambo had
made himself so competent in the busi-

ness and had proved himself worthy of trust, he determined to send Zambo to the fair, and bide at home himself and mind his shop.

After Zambo's departure it happened by ill fortune that Messer Ambros was seized with so grave and insidious an illness that after the lapse of a few days he died.   When his wife, who was called Madonna Felicetta, found that she was a widow, she wellnigh died herself, of grief[1] for the loss of her husband, and of anxiety on account of the breaking up of her business.   As soon as Zambo heard of the sad news of his master's death, he returned straightway and bore himself as a godly youth should, and diligently went about the affairs of the shop.   Madonna Felicetta, as time went on, re-marked that Zambo behaved himself well and uprightly, and was diligent over the business.   She considered, likewise, that a year had now rolled away since the death of Messer Ambros her hus-

[1] Orig., *anch ella no tira le calzi.*

band, and, as she feared to lose Zambo some day together with divers of the customers of her shop, she took counsel with some of her gossips whether she should marry or not, and in case she should resolve to marry, whether it would be well for her to take for a husband Zambo the factor of her business, who had been for a long time in the service of her first husband, and had gathered much experience in the conduct of her affairs. These worthy gossips deeming her proposition a wise one, counselled her to marry Zambo; and between the word and the deed but little time[1] intervened, for the nuptials were celebrated at once, and Madonna Felicetta became the wife of Ser Zambo and Ser Zambo the husband of Madonna Felicetta.

When Ser Zambo perceived himself raised to this high estate, how he had a wife of his own and a fine shop well stocked with all manner of cloth goods, he wrote to his father, telling him he

---

[1] Orig., *e dal dichg al fahg se fe le nozzi.*

was now in Rome, and of the great stroke of luck which had befallen him. The father, who since the day of Zambo's departure had heard no tidings of his son, nor had ever received a written word from him, now gave up the ghost from sheer joy, but Bertaz and Santì were mightily pleased and consoled with the news.

One day it chanced that Madonna Felicetta found herself in need of a new pair of stockings, because the ones she wore were rent and torn, wherefore she said to Ser Zambo her husband that he must have made for her another pair. To this Zambo replied that he had other business to do, and that if her stockings were torn, she had better go and mend them and patch them and put new heels thereto. Madonna Felicetta, who had been greatly pampered by her late husband, replied that it had never been her wont to go shod in hose which had been mended and heeled, and that she must have a new pair. Then answered Ser Zambo that in his country customs were different, and that she must do without. Thus the bout of wrangling began, and, flying from one angry word to another, it came to pass in the end that Ser Zambo lifted his hand and cuffed her over the head so heavily that she fell to the ground.[1] Madonna Felicetta, planning the while how she might give back these blows of Ser Zambo, was little disposed to come to terms with him or to pacify him in any way, so she began to hurl foul words at him. Ser Zambo, feeling that his honour was impugned thereby, belaboured her so soundly with his fists that the poor woman was constrained to hold her peace.

When the summer had passed, and the cold weather had set in, Madonna Felicetta asked Ser Zambo to let her have a silken lining wherewith to repair her pelisse, which was in very bad condition, and in order that he might be assured that she spoke the truth she

---

[1] Orig., *una mostazzada si fatta in sol mostaz, che la fe andà d'inturem.*

brought it to him to see ; but Ser Zambo did not trouble to cast his eye over it, but simply said that she must mend it and wear it as it was, for that in his country people were not used to so much pomp. Madonna Felicetta, when she heard these words, was mightily wroth, and affirmed that she must have granted to her what she asked at any cost. Ser Zambo, however, answered that she must hold her peace and be careful not to arouse his anger, otherwise it would be the worse for her. But Madonna Felicetta went on insisting that she must have it, and they one and the other worked themselves up into such a fury that they were well nigh blinded with rage. Whereupon Ser Zambo, according to his wont, began to thump her with his stick, and gave her as shrewd a jacketting of blows as she could bear, and she lay half dead.[1] When Madonna Felicetta saw how hugely Zambo's humour towards

[1] Orig., *e fag una pellizza de tanti bastonadi, quanti la ne pos mai portà, e la lassà quasi per morta.*

her had changed, she began to blas-
pheme and to curse the day and the hour
when she had first spoken to him, nor
did she forget those who had advised her
to take him for a husband. ' Is this the
way you treat me,' she cried, ' you pol-
troon, you ungrateful rascal, hangman,
Goth, and villainous scoundrel ? Is this
the reward you return to me for the many
benefits you have received ? for, from the
base hireling you formerly were, have I
not made you the master not only of
my wealth but of my person as well?
And yet you deal with me in this wise.
Hold your peace, traitor, for I will
make you pay smartly for this.' Ser
Zambo, hearing how his wife waxed
more and more wroth, and poured out
her abuse of him more copiously than
ever, made farther shrewd play upon
her back with his cudgel to give her a
finishing touch, whereupon Madonna
Felicetta was reduced to such a state
of fear, that when she heard the sound
of Zambo's voice or footstep, she trem-

bled like a leaf in the wind, and became all wet with terror.

When the winter had passed and the summer was coming on, it chanced that Ser Zambo had need to go to Bologna on account of business, and to collect certain sums of money due to him. As this journey would occupy some days, he said to Madonna Felicetta: 'Wife, I would have you know that I have two brothers, who are both hunchbacks as I am myself, and so closely do we all resemble one another that if anyone should see us all three together he would never know which was which. Now I bid you watch well lest they come here and attempt to lodge with us. See that you do not let them come over the threshold on any account, for they are wicked, deceitful, and crafty knaves, and would assuredly play you some evil trick. Then they would go to the devil and leave you with your hands full of flies.[1] If I should learn that you have harboured them in this house I will

---

[1] Orig., *che ti romagnis con le ma pieni de moschi.*

make you the most wretched woman in the world.' And having said these words he departed.

A few days after Zambo's departure the brothers Bertaz and Santì arrived, and went about asking for Ser Zambo's shop, which was pointed out to them. When the two rascals saw the fine shop, furnished richly with all manner of cloth goods, they were astounded, and marvelled amain how it was that he could have gathered together all this wealth in so short a time. And, lost in wonderment, they went to the shop and said they desired to have speech with Ser Zambo, but were told that he was gone into the country; if however, they had need of aught they could ask for it. Whereupon Bertaz said they much wished to speak with him, but as he was not at home they would speak with his wife, so they bade the servant call Madonna Felicetta, and when she came into the shop she knew at once that the men before her were her brothers-in-law. Bertaz, when he

saw her, straightway inquired of her,
'Madonna, are you the wife of Zambo?'
And she made answer that she was.
Then said Bertaz: 'Madonna, shake
hands, for we are the brothers of your
husband, and therefore your brothers-in-
law.' Madonna Felicetta, who well re-
membered the words of Ser Zambo as
well as the belabouring he had given her,
refused to touch their hands, but they
went on plying her with so many affec-
tionate words and gestures that in the end
she shook hands with them. As soon as
she had thus greeted them, Bertaz cried
out: 'Oh, my dear sister-in-law! give us
somewhat to eat, for we are half famished.'
But this she refused to do. The rogues,
however, knew so well how to use the
trick of flattery, and begged so persistently, that Madonna Felicetta was moved
to pity, and took them into the house
and gave them food and drink in plenty,
and even allowed them to sleep in a
certain corner. Scarcely had three days
passed since Bertaz and Santì had come

to Madonna Felicetta's house when Ser
Zambo returned. His wife, as soon as
she heard of this, was almost beside herself with terror, and she hardly knew
what to do so as to keep the brothers out
of Ser Zambo's sight, and as she could
hit upon no better plan she made them
go into the kitchen, where was a trough
in which they were accustomed to scald
pigs, and in this she bade them conceal
themselves.

When Ser Zambo entered the house
and marked how dishevelled and worried
his wife seemed to be, he was mightily upset in his mind and said: 'Why do you
look so frightened? What ails you? I
suppose there is no gallant hidden anywhere in the house?' But she replied in
a faint voice that there was nought the
matter with her. Ser Zambo, who was
regarding her sharply the while, said:
'Certes, there is something the matter
with you. Are those brothers of mine
by any chance in the house?' But she
answered boldly that they were not;

whereupon he began to give her a taste of the stick, according to his custom. Bertaz and Santi, who were under the pig-trough, could hear all the hurlyburly, and, so terrified were they, that they wet their breeches like children in a fright and did not venture to move. Ser Zambo, when he at last put down his stick, began to search the house in every corner to see whether he could find anyone hidden, but finding nought he calmed himself somewhat and went about the ordering of certain of his affairs, and so long was he occupied thereanent (thus keeping his luckless brothers in their hiding-place) that Bertaz and Santi, either through fear, or through the great heat, or on account of the foul stench of the pig-trough, straightway gave up the ghost.

When the hour had come at which Ser Zambo was wont to repair to the piazza, there to transact business with the other merchants, he went out of the house, and as soon as he had taken his departure Madonna Felicetta went to the pig-trough to devise some scheme for getting rid of her brothers-in-law, so that Ser Zambo might have no suspicion that she had given them shelter. But when she uncovered the trough she found them lying there both stark dead, and looking exactly like two pigs. The poor woman, when she saw what had happened, fell into a terrible taking of grief and despair, and, in order that her husband might be kept altogether in ignorance of what had occurred, she spent all her force in trying to throw them out of the house, so that the mishap might be hidden from Ser Zambo, and from all the rest of the city as well.

I have heard people say that in Rome there is a certain custom according to which, should the dead body of any stranger or pilgrim be found in the public streets or in any man's house, it is straightway taken up by certain scavengers[1] appointed for this purpose and car-

---

[1] Orig., *picegamort.*

ried by them outside the walls of the city
and then cast into the Tiber, so that of
such unfortunates nothing more is ever
heard or seen.   Now Madonna Felicetta,
having gone to look out of the window
to see whether by chance any friends of
hers might be passing by who would lend
aid in getting rid of the two dead bodies,
by good luck espied one of these corpse-
bearers, and called to him to come in,
telling him that she had a corpse in the
house, and that she wanted him to take
it away at once and cast it into the Tiber,
according to the custom of the place.
Already Madonna Felicetta had pulled
out one of the corpses from under the
cover of the trough, and had left it lying on the floor near thereto ; so, when
the corpse-bearer had come upstairs, she
helped him to load the dead body on his
shoulders, and bade him come back to
the house after he had thrown it into
the river, when she would pay him for
his services.   Whereupon the corpse-
bearer went outside the city wall and

threw the body into the Tiber, and, having done his work, he returned to Madonna Felicetta and asked her to give
him a florin, which was the customary
guerdon. But while the corpse-bearer
was engaged in carrying off the first body,
Madonna Felicetta, who was a crafty
dame, drew out from the trough the
other body and disposed it at the foot
of the trough in exactly the same place
where the first had lain, and when the
corpse-bearer came back to Madonna Felicetta for his payment, she said to him:
'Did you indeed carry the corpse I gave
you to the Tiber?' And to this the
fellow replied, 'I did, madonna.' 'Did
you throw it into the river?' said the
dame; and he answered: 'Did I throw
it in? indeed I did, and in my best
manner.' At this speech Madonna Felicetta said: 'How could you have
thrown it in, as you say you have?
Just look and see whether it be not still
here.' And when the corpse-bearer saw
the second dead body, he really thought

it must be the one he had carried away,
and was covered with dismay and confusion ; and, cursing and swearing the
while, he hoisted it upon his shoulders,
and, having carried it off, he cast it into
the Tiber, and stood for awhile to watch
it as it floated down the stream.[1]   And
whilst he was once more returning to
Madonna Felicetta's house to receive his
payment, it chanced that he met Ser
Zambo, who was on his way home, and
when the corpse-bearer espied the man
who bore so strong a likeness to the two
other hunchbacks whom he had carried
to the Tiber, he flew into such a violent
fit of rage that he seemed, as it were, to
spit forth fire and flames on all sides and
gave a free rein to his passion.   For in
truth he deemed the fellow before him to
be no other than the one whom he had
already twice cast into the river, and that
he must be some evil spirit who was returning to his own place; so he stole softly
behind Ser Zambo and dealt him a griev-

[1] Orig., *anda a segonda.*

ous blow on the head with an iron winch which he carried in his hand, saying: 'Ah! you cowardly, villainous loon, do you think that I want to spend the rest of my days in haling you to the river?' and as he thus railed he mishandled him so violently that poor Zambo, on account of the cudgelling he got, was soon a dead man and went to talk to Pilate.[1]

When the corpse-bearer had got upon his shoulders the third corpse, which was still warm, he bore it away and threw it into the Tiber after the two others, and thus Zambo and Bertaz and Santi miserably ended their lives. Madonna Felicetta, when she heard the news of this, was greatly delighted thereat, and felt no small content that she was freed from all her hardships and might again enjoy her former liberty.

Molino's fable here came to an end. It had pleased the ladies so mightily that they could not forbear from laughing thereat and talking it over. And

[1] Orig., *se n'anda a parla a Pilat.*

although the Signora more than once
bade them be silent, she found it no
easy matter to put an end to their merry
laughter.   At last, in order to bring the
company once more into a sedater mood,
she commanded Molino to set them to
guess an enigma in the same dialect, and
he, ever ready to obey her, gave his riddle in the following words:

> Out of their prison grave so dark
> Arise the bones of dead men stark,
> And 'twixt the hours of tierce and sext,
> By signs will tell to mortals vext
> What chance's smiles or frowns of fate
> May bless or ban till time grows late.
> Savage and deep the·misers curse,
> Making the signs of chance averse;
> But he, untouched by lust of gold,
> Unmoved will fortune's freaks behold.
> Next one with beard of flesh upsprings,
> And beak of bone, and warning sings
> To bid the watchers bury deep
> Their bodies in a downy sleep,
> And lie, poor fools by care unstirred,
> On welcome boon of foolish bird.

Though   Molino's   fable   forsooth

pleased the company much, this ingenious but somewhat gruesome enigma diverted them yet more; but forasmuch as
no one had gathered any inkling of its
meaning, the ladies with one voice begged
him earnestly that he should give the
solution thereof in the same dialect he
had used in his narration. Molino, when
he perceived that this was the general
wish of the company, in order that he
might not appear to be niggard of his
gifts, solved the enigma in the following
terms: " My enigma, dear ladies, signifies the game of hazard, and the bones
of the dead which leave their graves are
the dice which fall out of the dice-box,
and when they mark tray, deuce, and
ace, these are the points which show
good luck, and will not such points as
these put spirit into the play and money
into the purse of the man who often wins
the throw thereby? Does the loser ever
like to go away a loser, and does not all
this come by the change and variations
of fortune? The avaricious player who

always seeks to win will now and again
curse and swear so fiercely that I cannot
think why the earth does not open and
swallow him up.   And, at such times as
the game goes on all through the night,
the cock, who has a beard of flesh and
a beak of bone, will get up and crow
' Cock-a-doodle-do,' thus letting the
gamesters know that it is past midnight
and they ought to repair to their beds
of goose down.   When they lie in these
is it not like sinking into a deep grave?
Are you all content with this my explanation ? "

The explanation of this subtle enigma
was received by the whole company with
great laughter ; so hearty was it in sooth
that they could scarce forbear from roll-
ing about on their seats.   And after the
Signora had commanded everyone to
keep silent, she turned towards Molino
and said : " Signor Antonio, as the fair
orb of Dian outshines all other stars, so
the fable just told to us by you, together
with your enigma, bears off the palm

from all others which we have hitherto heard." Molino answered: "The praise you give me, Signora, cannot surely be due on account of my skill; it comes rather from the great courtesy which always abides in you. But if it should happen that the Trevisan were willing to tell you a story in the dialect of his country, I am sure you would listen to this with still greater pleasure." The Signora, who desired greatly to hear a story told in this fashion, said : " Signor Benedetto, do you hear what our Molino says? Certainly you would do him a great wrong were you to make false these words of his. Put, therefore, your hand in your pouch and draw therefrom some peasant story to enliven us all." The Trevisan, to whom it appeared unseemly that he should occupy the place of Arianna, whose turn came next, at first excused himself, but seeing that he could not weather [1] this point, began his fable in the following words.

[1] Orig., *schiffare tal scoglio.*

THE FOURTH FABLE.

Marsilio Vercelese, being enamoured of Thia, the wife of Cechato Rabboso, is taken by her into her house during her husband's absence. He having come back unexpected, is cozened by Thia, who feigns to work a spell, during which Marsilio silently takes to flight.[1]

IN good sooth, what more would you have, my lady mistress and fair damsels all? Has not Messer Antonio acquitted himself well? Has he not told you an excellent story? But, by the blood of a dog, I will do my best to match him, and to gather the best credit I may.

We villagers have always heard tell, that amongst gentlemen of the world, one man will manage his affairs in this way, and another in that. But I, who am an ignorant loon, and who know nothing of letters, tell you what I have always heard said by our elders, namely, that he who dances badly raises the loud-

[1] Told in the dialect of Treviso.

est laugh;[1] so if you will have patience,
I will do my best to amuse you. But
do not think that I say these words because I wish to escape the trouble of telling you a tale, for I am not in the least
fearful on this score. And, over and
beyond this, I would have you understand that the story which Messer Antonio has told you, with so good a grace
that it would be hard to beat, has fired
me with so much courage that now, when
I see I am indeed launched on my task,
it seems to me a thousand years until I
shall be able to begin. Perhaps indeed
this fable of mine will be no less pleasing and laughable than Messer Antonio's, especially as I purpose to tell you
of the ingenuity of a peasant woman who
played a trick upon her fool of a husband; wherefore, if you will listen to me
and give me your kind attention, I will
tell it to you as well as I can.

Above the domain of Piove de Sacco,
which is, as I need hardly tell you, a

---

[1] Orig., *chi mal balla, ben solassa.*

territory of Padua, seeing that this must
be well known to all of you, is situated
a village called Salmazza, wherein there
lived, a very long time since, a peasant
called Cechato Rabbóso, who, although
he was a fellow with a big head and
body, was nevertheless a poor fool and
over-trustful of his own powers. This
Cechato Rabboso had to wife the daughter of a farmer called Gagiardi, who lived
in a village called Campelongo, and she
was a wily, crafty, and mischievous young
woman, called by the name of Thia.
Besides being so shrewd, she was in her
person a stout wench and handsome of
face, so that it was commonly said there
was not another peasant woman for miles
round who could be compared with her.
And because she was so sprightly and
nimble at country dances, the young
gallants who saw her would not seldom
lose their hearts to her straightway.
Now it happened that a certain young
man, who was himself handsome and of
a sturdy figure, a prosperous citizen of

Padua, by name Marsilio Vercelese, became enamoured of this Thia, and so
ardently was he consumed by the flame
of his love that whenever she went to a
village dance this youth would be sure
to follow her thither, and for the greater
part of the time he would dance with
her, devoting himself entirely to her and
never dancing with any other woman.
But although this young gallant was so
fiercely enamoured of her, he kept his
love a secret as well as he could, so as
not to let it be known to anybody, nor
to become a matter of common gossip
to all the neighbours round about.

Marsilio, knowing quite well that
Cechato, Thia's husband, was a poor
man, supporting his house by the work
of his hands, and from the early morning till late at night labouring hard, now
at this, now at that work, began to prowl
about Thia's house, and, by constantly
plying her with soft glances, he soon
found an opportunity of addressing her.
Now, although Marsilio had determined

in his mind to disclose the love which he bore her, still he doubted whether she might not be angered and refuse to see him again in case he should declare his passion, for it did not seem to him that she looked upon him so kindly as he deserved, seeing how great was the love he had for her. And, besides this, he was afraid of being discovered. by some malicious person who would caution Cechato her husband, who on this account might very likely do him some evil turn; for Cechato, although he was such a numskull, was sharp enough to be jealous.

Marsilio, therefore, spent his days in assiduously haunting the house where Thia lived, and he would gaze at her so long and so intently that at last she could not fail to be aware that he was enamoured of her. But, for certain reasons best known to herself, she forbore to look favourably upon him, or show that she was in any way inclined to return his passion, and although she was

in her secret mind quite willing to meet
his wishes, she feigned to be indifferent
to him, and turned her back upon him.

One day it chanced that Thia was sitting all alone on a wooden bench placed
near the outer door of the house, and
holding under her arm the distaff on
which some flax was wound — she was,
indeed, busy doing some spinning for
her landlady — when Marsilio, who had
taken a little heart of grace, came forward and said to her : ' God be with you,
my friend Thia ! ' And Thia answered :
' Welcome, young gentleman ! ' ' How
is it that you do not know,' said Marsilio, ' that I am consumed of love for
you, and am like to die, and you on
your part make no account of it, and
care not in the least about my cruel
sufferings ? ' To this Thia answered :
' How should I know whether you love
me or not ? ' Said Marsilio : ' If you
never knew it before, I will now let you
know that such is my case, for I am
consumed with all the grief and passion

that a man can feel.' And Thia answered him : 'Well, of a surety you have let me know it now.' Then Marsilio said, 'And you? Ah, tell me the truth, by the faith you have! Do you love me too?' Thia, with a smile answered, 'Perhaps I love you a little.' Then said Marsilio, 'Heaven help you, tell me how much?' 'I love you very much,' answered Thia. Then Marsilio cried, 'Alas, Thia! if you really loved me as much as you say, you would show it to me by some sign, but I cannot believe that you love me at all.' Thia answered, 'Well, and what sign would you have me give you?' 'Oh, Thia!' said Marsilio, 'you know very well what is in my mind without my telling you.' 'No, I cannot possibly know it unless you tell me,' said Thia. Then Marsilio replied, 'I will tell you if you will listen to me, and not be angered.' Thia then answered, 'Say on, sir, for I promise you on my soul that, if it is a good thing and not against my honour, I will not

be angered with you.' Then Marsilio
said, 'Then, my love, when will you give
me the chance of holding you in my arms
in lover's fashion?' 'I now see clearly
enough,' said Thia, 'that you are only
deceiving me, and making a mock of me.
How can I be fitted for you, who are a
gentleman and a citizen of Padua, whilst
I am a peasant of the village? You are
rich, and I am poor; you are a signor,
and I am a working woman; you can
have fine ladies to your taste, and I am
of low condition. You are wont to walk
gaily with your embroidered surcoat, and
your bright-coloured hose, all worked
with wool and silk, and I, as you see,
have nought but a dimity petticoat, old,
torn, and mended. I have nothing better
when I go to dances than this old gar-
ment and this linen head-cloth. You
eat wheaten loaves, and I rye-bread and
beans and polenta, and even then I have
often not enough to satisfy my hunger.
I have no pelisse for the cold winter,
poor wretch that I am! nor do I know

which way to turn to get one, for I have
neither money nor goods to sell that will
enable me to buy the few necessaries that
I want. We have not enough corn to eat
to keep us alive till Easter, and I know
not what we shall do during the great
dearth. And besides all this, there are
the forced dues that we have to pay to
Padua every day. Oh, we poor peasants!
what pleasure have we in life? We
toil hard to till the earth and to sow our
wheat, which you fine folk consume,
whilst we poor people have to make the
best shift we can with rye-bread. We
tend the vines and make the wine, of
which you drink the best, and we have
to be satisfied with wine lees or water.'

In answer to Thia's speech Marsilio
said: 'Do not distress yourself on account of this, for if you grant me the
favour I desire I will see that you want
for nothing that can give you delight.'
Thia replied: 'Ah! this is what you
cavaliers always say until we have done
your pleasure; then you go away and

we never see any more of you, and, fools
as we are, are left in the lurch, deceived
and duped and shamed in the world's
esteem. You, meantime, go your ways,
bragging of your good fortune and wash-
ing out your mouths, as far as concerns
us, and all that belongs to us,[1] treating
us as if we were carrion only fit to be
cast out on the dunghill. I know full
well the tricks you worthy citizens of
Padua can play.' Then said Marsilio:
'Enough, now let us have done with
words for good and all. I ask you once
more whether you will grant me the
favour I desire?' 'Go away, for the
love of God, I pray you,' cried Thia,
'before my husband comes back, for
nightfall is drawing near and he will certainly be here in a few minutes. Come
back some time to-morrow, and we will
talk as long as you will, for in sooth I
love you well.' But Marsilio, who was
indeed passionately in love with her, was

---

[1] Orig., *V'ande laldando, e lavando la bocca di fatti
nuostri.*

loath to leave off this pleasant conversation, and still remained by her side; so
she said once more, 'Go away immediately, I beg you, and do not stay here
any longer.' When Marsilio saw that
Thia was thus strongly moved, he cried
out, 'God be with you, Thia, my sweet
soul! I recommend my heart to you,
for it is surely in your keeping.' 'May
God go with you, dearest hope of my
life!' said Thia, 'I commend you to
His care.' 'By His good help,' said
Marsilio, 'we will meet again to-morrow.' 'Very well, let it be so,' said
Thia; and with these words Marsilio
took his leave.

When the morrow had come Marsilio, to whom the time until he should
once more repair to Thia's house seemed
a thousand years, went thither forthwith
and found her busy in the garden dig-
ging and mulching round about certain
vines which grew therein, and as soon
as they saw one another they exchanged
greetings and began to talk lovingly to-

gether. And when this conversation had gone on for some time Thia said to Marsilio : ' Dear heart of mine, tomorrow morning early Cechato my husband will have occasion to go to the mill, and he will not return hither until the next day ; wherefore, if it should be your pleasure, you may come here late in the evening. I will be on the watch for you ; only be sure that you come without fail, and do not deceive me.' When Marsilio heard this good news, there was no man in all the world so happy as he was ; he jumped and danced about for very gladness, and took leave of Thia, half out of his wits for joy.

As soon as Cechato had come home, the crafty Thia went up to him and said, 'Cechato, my good man, you must needs go to the mill straightway, for we have nothing more in the house to eat.' ' Very well, very well, I will see about it,' answered Cechato. ' I tell you that you must go to-morrow, whatever happens,' said Thia. ' Very well, then,' replied Cechato, 'to-morrow morning before I go I will. borrow a cart with two oxen from the people for whom I work, then I will come back to load it, and go off to the mill at once.'

In the meantime Thia went to prepare the corn and to put it into sacks, so that on the morrow Cechato should have nothing to do but to load his cart therewith, and to go on his way singing. On the following morning Cechato took the corn which his wife had put into sacks the night before, and loaded it on the cart and went on his way towards the mill. And seeing that it was now the season of short days and long nights, and that the roads were broken up and in bad condition, and that the weather was foul with rain and ice and intense cold, poor Cechato found himself obliged to remain that night at the mill, and this in sooth fell in most opportunely with the plans that Thia and Marsilio had devised for their own satisfaction.

As soon as the dark night had fallen,

Marsilio, according to the agreement he
had made with Thia, took a pair of
fine well-cooked capons and some white
bread and wine unspoilt by any drop of
water therein, all of which he had carefully prepared before he left his home,
and stole secretly across the fields to
Thia's house. Then, having opened the
door, he found her sitting by the fireside winding thread. After greeting one
another they spread the table and both
sat down to eat, and after they had made
an excellent meal off Marsilio's good
cheer, they went to lie down in the bed;
thus, whilst that poor fool of a Cechato
was having his corn ground at the mill,
in his bed at home Marsilio was sifting
flour.

When the time of sunrise was near,
and the day was beginning to break, the
two lovers awoke and rose from their bed,
fearing lest Cechato might return and
find them there together; but while they
were still amorously talking, Cechato
drew near to the house, whistling aloud

the while, and calling upon Thia, saying: 'Oh, my Thia! make up a good
fire, I pray you, for I am more than half
dead with cold.' Thia, who was a clever,
artful minx, was somewhat frightened
when she heard her husband's voice, and
feared amain lest some evil should befall
Marsilio, and injury and shame be put
upon herself; so she quickly opened the
door, managing the while to allow Marsilio to hide himself behind it; then with
a merry face she ran to meet her husband, and began to embrace him. And
after Cechato had come into the courtyard, he cried out once more to his wife:
'Make a fire at once, good Thia, for I
am wellnigh frozen to death. By the
blood of St. Quintin, I was almost
starved to death by cold last night up
at that mill; so cold was it, indeed, that
I was not able to sleep a wink or even
to close an eye.' Whereupon Thia went
without delay to the wood-house, and
having taken therefrom a good armful
of billets she lighted a fire whereat

Cechato might warm himself, herself occupying craftily that spot by the hearth
from whence Marsilio might perchance
be seen by Cechato.

Then Thia, chatting with her husband
of this and of that, said: 'Ah! Cechato,
my good man, I have a fine bit of news
to give you.' 'What has happened?'
inquired Cechato. To this Thia replied,
'Whilst you were away at the mill a
poor old man came to the house begging
alms of me for the love of God, and as
a recompense for some bread I gave him
to eat and a small cup of wine, he taught
me an incantation wherewith to throw a
spell over that greedy kite which often
comes hereabouts, and never in my life
have I heard anything more beautiful
than his words, which I have learnt well
by heart.' 'What is this thing you are
telling me?' said Cechato; 'is it really
the truth?' Thia replied, 'It is true, by
my faith, and I can tell you that I set
great store by it.' 'Then tell it to me
at once,' said Cechato, 'and do not hold

me longer in suspense.' Whereupon
Thia said to her husband, 'You must
lie down flat on the ground stretched
out your full length, just as if you were
dead (which thing may God avert!), and
having done this you must turn your
head and your shoulders towards the
door, and your knees and feet towards
the stove, and then I must spread a
white cloth over your face, and put our
corn measure over your head.'

'But I am quite sure,' said Cechato,
'that my head will never go into our
corn measure.'   'I am sure it will,' replied Thia; 'just look here!'   And with
these words she took the measure, which
happened to be close at hand, and put
it over his head, saying, 'Nothing in
God's world could be a better fit than
this.   And now you must keep yourself
quite still, neither moving a limb nor
saying a word, otherwise we shall be able
to do nothing.   Then I will take our
tamis sieve in my hand, and will begin
to jump and dance around you, and

whilst I am thus dancing I will speak
the incantation which the old man taught
me.   And in this fashion the spell may
be well and truly worked.   But again I
tell you that you must on no account stir
a finger until I shall have repeated the
incantation thrice, for it must be said
three times over you in order that it may
have any effect.   After this we shall see
whether the kite gives us any more trouble, or comes to steal our chicken.'   To
this Cechato replied : ' Would to God
that what you say might be true, so that
we might have a little rest and breathing
space.   You know well enough how hard
we find it to bring up any chicken at all,
on account of that fiend of a kite which
devours every one we hatch.   Never
have we been able to rear enough chicken
to sell, and with the money gained thereby
to pay our landlord and the tax-gatherer,
and to buy oil and salt and any other
stores we may want for housekeeping.'

' Let us begin quickly then,' said
Thia, ' for in this fashion we shall be

able to do ourselves a good turn. Now, Cechato, lie down quickly.' And Cechato straightway laid himself down on the floor. 'Now stretch yourself out well to your full length,' said Thia. And Cechato at once did his best to stretch himself out as far as ever he could.

'That is right,' said Thia, and hereupon she took a cloth of thick white linen and shrouded his face therewith. Next she took the corn measure and rammed it down on his head, and then caught up the tamis sieve and began to dance and skip around him and to repeat in the following wise the incantation which she said had been taught her by the old beggar:

> Thievish bird, I charge you well,
> Hearken to my mystic spell.
> While I dance and wave my sieve,
> All my tender chicks shall live.
> Not a bird from all my hatch,
> Thievish rascal, shall you snatch.
> Wolf nor rat his prey shall seek,
> Nor bird with sharp and crooked beak.

The Incantation Of Cecha
Rabboso By This

Night the Fifth

FOURTH FABLE

The Incantation Of Cechato Rabboso By Thia

Night the Fifth

FOURTH FABLE

The Incantation Of Cachate

The Incantation Of Cechato Rabboso By Thia

———

𝕹𝖎𝖌𝖍𝖙 𝖙𝖍𝖊 𝕱𝖎𝖋𝖙𝖍

FOURTH FABLE

The Incantation Of Cechato
Rabbaso By Thir

Night the Fifth

The Incantation Of Cechato
Rabboso By Thia

———

Night the Fifth

FOURTH FABLE

Thieves who stand-behind the door,
Hearken, fly, and come no more.
If my speech you cannot read,
Surely you are fools indeed.

When Thia had come to the end of
her mummery she still went on dancing
round Cechato, keeping her eyes fixed
upon the outer door the while, and making signs to Marsilio, who was there con-
cealed, that he had better run away at
once.   But Marsilio, who was neither
nimble-minded nor quick to catch her
meaning, failed to comprehend what
might be the purport of the gestures she
was making or what she meant by going
through these rites of exorcism; so he
kept still in his hiding-place and did not
budge an inch.   Meantime Cechato, being now half stifled and mightily weary
of lying stretched out on the floor, was
anxious to get up, and spake thus to
Thia: 'Well, is it all over now?'   But
Thia, who had not been able to induce
Marsilio to move from his place behind
the door, answered Cechato in these

words: 'Stay where you are, for heaven's sake, and move not at your peril. Did I not tell you that I should have to repeat the incantation three times? I hope you may not have wrecked everything, as it is, by wanting to get up.' 'No, no, surely not,' said Cechato. And Thia made him lie down stretched out as he was before, and began to chant her incantation anew.

Now by this time Marsilio had at last come to understand how matters really stood, and what was the meaning of Thia's mummery, so he seized the opportunity to slip out from his hiding-place, and to run away as fast as his legs could carry him. Thia, when she saw Marsilio take to his heels and run out of the courtyard, finished her form of exorcism against the kite, and when she had brought it to an end she suffered her cuckoldly fool of a husband to get up from the ground. Then with Thia's help he began forthwith to unload the flour which he had brought back from

the mill.   Now Thia when she went
with Cechato outside into the courtyard
to help unload the flour, saw Marsilio in
the distance hurrying away at the top of
his speed, whereupon she began to shout
after him in a lusty voice: 'Ah, ah!
What a wicked bird!   Ah, ah! begone,
get away!   For, by my faith, I will send
you packing with your tail between
your legs if ever you show yourself here
again.   Away then, I tell you!   Is not
he a greedy wretch?   Do you not see
that the wicked beast was bent on coming
back?   Heaven give him a bad year!'

And in this fashion it happened, that
every time the kite came and flew down
into the courtyard to carry away a chick
or two, he would first have a bout with
the hen herself,[1] who would afterwards
set to work with her conjuration as before.   Then he would take to flight with
his tail down, but all the while the fowls
belonging to Cechato and Thia suffered
no damage at all from his harrying.

[1] Orig., *in prima el se spellatava con la chiozza.*

This fable, given by the Trevisan, was found to be so mirthful and amusing that the ladies, and the gentlemen as well, almost split their sides with laughter; so well did he mock the rustic speech that there was no one of the company who would not have judged him to be a peasant of Treviso. And when the merriment had abated somewhat, the Signora turned her fair face towards the Trevisan and spake to him thus: " In truth, Signor Benedetto, you have this evening diverted us in such featly wise that with one voice we declare your fable may deservedly be held to be the equal of Molino's in merit. But to fill up the measure of my content and that of this honourable company, I entreat you — an it displease you not — that you will set forth to us an enigma which shall be as graceful in form as amusing in matter." The Trevisan, when he saw how the Signora was inclined, was unwilling to disappoint her; so, standing up, with a clear voice and with no hesitation of

any sort, he began his riddle in the following words :

> Sir Yoke goes up and down the field,
> To every tug is forced to yield.
> One on the left, one on the right
> Plods on, and next there comes a wight,
> A cunning rascal who with power
> Beats one who goes on carriers four.
> Now if an answer you can give,
> Good friends, we will for ever live.

When the Trevisan, with the true
manner and bearing of a peasant, had
finished his enigma, which was comprehended by few or none of the company,
he thus gave the interpretation thereof
in peasant dialect in order that its meaning might be made clear to them all :
" I must not keep this gentle company
waiting any longer. Tell me, do you
understand the meaning of my enigma?
If you do not know, I will tell you.
Sir Yoke goes to and fro, that is to say,
the yoke, to which the oxen are attached,
goes up and down the fields and roads,

and is dragged hither and thither by them. Those who fare, the one on this side and the other on that side of it, are the oxen. He who beats one who stands on four, means that the plough-man who walks behind lashes the bull, who has four legs, with his leathern whip. And to end my explanation, I tell you once more that the answer to my riddle is the yoke, and I hope you will all understand it."

Everyone was greatly interested over this riddle dealing with country life, and, laughing heartily thereat, they praised it highly. But the Trevisan, remembering that only one more story remained to be told this night, to wit, that of the charming Cateruzza, turned with a smiling face towards the Signora and spake thus: "Signora, it is not for the reason that I wish to disturb the settled order of this our entertainment, or to dictate to your highness, my mistress and sovereign lady, but merely to satisfy the desire of this devoted company, that I

beg your excellency to make us the shar-
ers of some fair fancies of your own, by
telling us, for our delight and recreation,
a story with your wonted grace. And
if I peradventure have been more presumptuous (which God forbid) in making this request than is suitable to my
humble estate, I beg you will forgive
me, seeing that the love I bear towards
this gracious assembly has been the chief
cause why I have been led to prefer it."

The Signora, when she heard the courteous petition of the Trevisan, at first
cast her eyes down upon the ground;
not, however, for any fear or shame that
she felt, but because she deemed that, for
divers reasons, it was more seemly for
her to listen than to discourse. But after
a time, with a gracious and smiling look,
as if her humour were a merry one, she
turned her bright face towards the Trevisan and said : " Signor Benedetto, what
though your request is a pleasant and
seemly one, it appears to me that you
are somewhat too insistent a beggar,

forasmuch as the duty of story-telling
pertains rather to these young damsels
round about than to me ; therefore you
must hold me excused if I decline to give
way at once to your demand, and bid
Cateruzza, who has been chosen by lot
to tell the fifth story of this evening, to
favour you with her discourse." The
merry listeners, who were mightily eager
to hear the Signora tell her story, forthwith all rose to their feet and began to
support the request of the Trevisan,
begging her most earnestly that she
would in this matter favour them with
her courtesy and kindness, and not stand
too severely by the exalted dignity of
her position, for time and place will allow anyone, however high in rank, to
speak freely whatever thing may be
pleasing. The Signora, when she heard
the gentle loving terms of this petition,
in order that she might not seem ungra-
cious in her bearing, smilingly replied :
" Since this is the wish of all of you, and
your pleasure withal, that I should con-

clude this evening with some little story
of my own, I will gladly grant your
wish." And without further demur she
blithely began to tell her fable.

THE FIFTH FABLE.

**Madonna Modesta, wife of Messer Tristano
Zanchetto, in her young days gathers together
a great number of shoes, offerings made by
her various lovers. Having grown old, she
disposes of the same to divers servants, bar-
lets, and other folk of mean estate.**

IT commonly happens that ill-
gotten wealth, and indeed all
riches which have been acquired by evil ways, are scat-
ered abroad and dissipated in brief space
of time, for by the divine will it has been
decreed that, quickly as such riches come,
quickly they shall depart This, indeed,
proved to be the case with a certain woman of Pistoia, who, had she been honest
and wise in the same degree as she was
dissolute and foolish, would never have
given occasion for the story which I am

now about to tell to you. And although perhaps this fable of mine is one hardly suitable for your ears, forasmuch as it comes to an end in a picture of shame and dishonour, which obscures and tarnishes the fame of those who live honest lives, nevertheless I will not hesitate to relate it to you, for at the right time and place it may serve (I speak here to those to whom it may apply) as a useful incentive for all to pursue the ways of uprightness and well-doing, and to eschew all wicked courses and lewd inclinations.

I must first tell this worshipful company that, not far from these our days, there lived in Pistoia, an ancient city of Tuscany, a young woman called by name Madonna Modesta, but this name, on account of her reprehensible manner of life and the shameful courses she followed, was one in no wise befitting her. In person, indeed, this woman was very lovely and graceful, though she was of mean condition.

She had a husband called Tristano

Zanchetto[1] (a name as well suited to him as his wife's was unfitting to her), a good-tempered fellow, given to merry company, and thinking of little else save of his business of buying and selling, whereby he gained a good living for himself. Madonna Modesta, who was by nature of a lecherous temper, and inclined for nought else but amorous sport, when she saw that her husband was given up heart and soul to commerce, and careful only about the matters appertaining thereto, took it into her head that she too would embark in merchandise and set up a new trade, concerning which her husband, Messer Tristano, should know nothing.

Wherefore every day she was wont to go out upon the balcony for her amusement, now on one side, now on the other, and throw glances at any gallant who might be passing in the street, and when her eye might chance to fall upon anyone whose appearance pleased her,

[1] *Zanchetto, zannetto,* a buffoon, a zany.

she would strive by divers suggestive
signs and gestures to arouse his curiosity
and desire, and to lure him to her.   And
in the course of time it proved that
Madonna Modesta had no mean skill in
the art of traffic; indeed, so diligent was
she in the display of her merchandise,
and so carefully did she attend to the
needs of her customers, that there was
to be found in all the city no one, rich
or poor, noble or plebeian, who was not
anxious to take and taste of her goods.
When, therefore, Madonna Modesta had
attained a position of great notoriety in
her calling, and had gathered together
much wealth thereby, she made up her
mind to exact only a very small guerdon
from anyone who might come to her as
a claimant for her favours.   That is to
say, she made it her custom to demand
from her lovers no greater reward than
a pair of shoes, stipulating, however,
that each one should give shoes of a sort
such as he might in an ordinary way
wear himself.   Thus, if the lover who

had been with her happened to be a
noble, she would expect from him a pair
of velvet shoes ; if a burgher, she would
ask for a pair of shoes made of fine cloth :
if a mechanic, a pair made of leather.
So great a concourse of clients flocked
to this good woman's place of business
that it was rarely or never empty, and
seeing that she was young and beautiful
and of fine figure, seeing likewise that the
price which she demanded for her favours was such a modest one, all the men
of Pistoia freely repaired to her house
and took their pleasure therein. At the
time of which I am writing, Madonna
Modesta had already filled a very large
storehouse with shoes, the wealth she had
gathered together in her tender amorous
calling, and so mighty was the tale of
shoes of every sort and quality, that if
any man here in Venice had searched
diligently every shop in the city he
would not have found a third part of the
number of shoes which Madonna Modesta had heaped up in her storehouse.

It happened one day that Messer Tristano her husband had need to use this same storehouse for the stowing away of certain chattels and merchandise which by chance had been consigned to him at the same time from divers parts of the world; so, having called Madonna Modesta his beloved wife, he asked her to hand over to him the keys of the warehouse. And she, like the crafty jade that she was, presented them to him without excuse of any sort; and the husband, when he opened the storehouse, which he expected would be empty, found it quite full of shoes (as has already been told) of divers qualities. When he saw this he was mightily astonished thereat, and could in no wise understand whence had come this great quantity of shoes of all sorts; so, having called his wife, he put a question to her as to where these shoes with which his warehouse was filled had come from. To this the astute Madonna Modesta answered in these words: ' What think you of this, good Messer

Tristano my husband? Did you in sooth
set yourself down as the only merchant
in this city? Certes, if you did, you were
hugely mistaken, for be sure that we
women likewise know somewhat concerning the art of traffic; and, although you
may be a great merchant, accustomed to
concern yourself with many and weighty
ventures, I content myself with commerce on a smaller scale. Wherefore I
have stored my merchandise in this warehouse, and put it safely under lock and
key in order that it may be kept secure.
So I beg you to keep your care and watch-
fulness for the benefit of your own goods
and your own traffic, and I will do the
same with regard to mine.' Messer Tristano, who knew nothing more than what
his wife told him, and asked no further
questions, was gratified amain with the
exceeding ingenuity and great foresight
of his clever and far-seeing wife, and besought her to prosecute with diligence
the enterprise she had undertaken. Madonna Modesta therefore continued in

secret to carry on her amorous trade, and, as in the exercise thereof she prospered mightily, she gathered together so vast a store of shoes that she could have easily supplied the wants not only of Pistoia, but of any other great city as well.

Thus whilst Madonna Modesta remained young and full of grace and beauty her trade showed no sign of falling off. But in the process of years cruel Time, the master of all things and all men, who fixes ever a beginning, a middle, and an end for all, so dealt with Madonna Modesta, who had been heretofore fresh and plump and lovely, that he changed the semblance of her face, and of her hair [1] likewise — leaving her desire unsubdued the while — and traced many wrinkles upon her forehead, and disfigured her countenance. Her eyes became rheumy and her breasts all dry and empty as shrivelled bladders, and

---

[1] Orig., *e mutò le usate penne.* The use of *penne* or *piume* for *capelli* is not uncommon. Thus in Dante, " Che riavèsse le maschile penne " (*Inferno*, xx.): " Movendo quell' oneste piume " (*Purgatorio*, i.).

whenever she happened to smile the skin
of her face became so puckered that anyone who looked at her was fain to laugh
and hold her in ridicule. And when the
time came that Madonna Modesta was
grown old and grey-headed, and lovers
no longer sought her to pay court to her
as formerly, she found that she added no
more shoes to her store, and she lamented
bitterly in her heart thereanent. From
the first years of her youth until the
present hour she had given herself over
entirely to the vice of luxury, the de-
structive enemy of the body and of the
purse as well, and she had likewise become more accustomed to dainty living
and libidinous life than any other woman
in the world, therefore she could find no
method or means by which she might
withdraw herself from these noxious ways.
And although in her body, from day to
day, the vital fluid, through which all
plants and living things take root and
grow, failed more and more, nevertheless the desire of satisfying her wicked

and unrestrained appetite was as violent
as ever. Therefore Madonna Modesta,
seeing that she was entirely bereft of
youthful beauty, and was no longer one
to be flattered and caressed by handsome
young gallants as in former days, made
up her mind to order her plans anew.
For the furtherance of these she once
more went out upon the balcony, and
began to ogle and to spread her lures to
catch any varlets or porters or peasants
or chimney-sweepers or idle fellows of
any sort, who might be passing by, and
any of these whom she might attract she
would entice into her house for her own
purposes, and with them take such pleasure as she had hitherto been wont to take.
And as in times past she had always demanded from each one of her lovers a
pair of shoes of a quality according with
the donor's condition as the reward for
her favours granted, now, on the other
hand, she found herself obliged to give a
pair of shoes from her stock to anyone
who would come to her. Madonna Mo-

desta had now sunk into such a shameful state that all the lowest ruffians of Pistoia would betake themselves to her dwelling, some to have their pleasure of her, others to make mock of her and to befool her, and others to receive the disgraceful guerdon which she was wont to give.

In this manner of life pursued by Madonna Modesta, it came to pass that the storehouse, which had once been crammed full of shoes, became wellnigh void. Messer Tristano one day, having a mind to go by stealth and see how his wife was prospering in her commerce, and whether her store of merchandise was increasing, took the key of the warehouse without his wife's knowledge and opened the door, only to find, when he looked in, that nearly all the shoes were gone. Wherefore Messer Tristano was beyond measure amazed, for he could not understand how his wife could have disposed of the many pairs of shoes he had formerly seen there. On this account he began to fancy that by this time his wife must, as it were, be made of gold by reason of her prosperous traffic, and he felt himself mightily consoled at the thought; for he deemed that he might hereafter be a sharer in her wealth.   So he straightway called her to him and thus addressed her: 'Modesta, I have always rated you as a wise and prudent woman, but this day I chanced to open your storehouse, wishing to see how your commerce was thriving, and deeming that by this time your stock of shoes must have greatly increased, but I found, instead of any increase, that your wares had nearly all disappeared.   At first I was mightily astonished thereat, but afterwards it came into my mind that you must have trafficked them away and received therefor a great sum of money, whereupon I was greatly reassured, and if this notion of mine should prove to be correct I shall hold that you have traded at great profit.'

Madonna Modesta, when her husband

had finished his speech, heaved a deep
sigh and thus made answer to him:
'Messer Tristano, my husband, do not
be amazed at what you have lately seen,
for I must tell you that all those shoes
you saw some long time ago in my warehouse, have walked away in the same
fashion in which they came to me. And
over and above this let me tell you that
those things which are ill got will, for
the most part, ill go in a very brief space
of time. Therefore I bid you once more
not to wonder or be surprised at what
you have seen.' Messer Tristano, who
did not in any way fathom the meaning
of his wife's words, fell into a great state
of fright and confusion, fearing hugely
lest a similar mischance might befall the
goods and merchandise he himself had
collected. However, he forebore to discuss the matter with her farther, but
bestirred himself anxiously to see that
his own merchandise might not vanish
as his wife's had vanished.

Madonna Modesta finding herself now

slighted by men of all sorts and conditions, and entirely beggared of all the
shoes she had gained in the course of
her lecherous youth, fell into a grave
malady, and in a very brief space of time
died miserably of consumption.   And in
this manner Madonna Modesta, who
took so little heed for the future, made
a shameful end of her life and also of the
possessions she had gathered together,
leaving nothing behind her to serve as
an example to the rest of the world, but
rather a disgraceful memory.

When the Signora had ended her
short fable all the company began to
laugh aloud, and heaped abundant blame
upon Madonna Modesta, who lived
moderately enough in all things save
only in the matter of lecherous indulgence.   And again they could not help
laughing when they recalled to mind the
story of the shoes which were so easily
got and so easily spent.   But because
it was on Cateruzza's account that the
Trevisan had urged the Signora to tell

this fable, the latter now began to spur
on the damsel with words which, though
gently spoken, had a sting therein, and
afterwards, as a penalty for having failed
to tell her fable, expressly commanded
Cateruzza to propound an enigma which
should not be irrelevant to the subject
of the fable they had just heard. Wherefore Cateruzza, when she heard the
command of the Signora, rose from her
seat, and turning herself towards her
spake thus: "Dear Signora, the biting
rebukes which you have just addressed
to me are not in any way displeasing to
me; on the contrary, I gladly take them
home to myself with my whole heart.
But the task of making my enigma agree
in some measure with the fable you have
just told us is no light one, seeing that
I am entirely unprepared. Since, however, it pleases you to punish in this
fashion my fault, if indeed it be a fault,
I, as an obedient girl and your most
complaisant handmaiden, will begin at
once.

My lady seats her in a chair,
And raises then her skirts with care;
And as I know she waits for me,
I bring her what she fain would see.
Then soft I lift her dainty leg,
Whereon she cries, 'Hold, hold, I beg!
It is too strait, and eke too small;
Be gentle, or you'll ruin all.'
And so to give her smallest pain,
I try once more, and eke again."

The enigma told by Cateruzza provoked as great laughter as the ingenious
fable which the Signora had recently
given; but, for the reason that certain
of the listeners put thereupon a somewhat lewd interpretation, she set herself
at once to make the honesty of her intent clear to them in as civil terms as
she could use: " Noble ladies, the real
subject of my enigma is nothing greater
or less than a tight shoe; for when the
lady has sat down, the shoemaker, with
the shoe in his hand, raises her foot,
whereupon she tells him to put the shoe
on gently, as it is too tight, and causes
her much pain.   Then he takes it off

and puts it on again and again till it fits
her well, and she is content therewith."

When the explication of Cateruzza's
enigma had been brought to an end and
highly praised by the whole company,
the Signora, seeing that the hour was
now late, gave order that under pain of
her displeasure no one should leave the
place, and, having bidden them summon
into her presence the trusty steward of
the household, she directed him to set
out the tables in the great hall. And
while the feast was in course of prep-
aration she proposed that the ladies
and gentlemen should divert themselves
with the dance, and, after the dance was
finished, they sang two songs. Then
the Signora rose to her feet and went
into the supper room, having the Signor
Ambassador on one hand and Messer
Pietro Bembo on the other, the rest
of the company following in their due
order. And when they had washed their
hands, each one sat down according to
his rank at the table, which was richly

spread with rare and delicate dishes and new wines.   When this merry feast had come to end amidst the loving discourse of the guests, each one being in blither mood than ever, they rose from the board and forthwith began to sing and dance in a circle.   But forasmuch as the rosy light of dawn was now beginning to appear, the Signora bade the servants to kindle the torches and go in attendance on the Signor Ambassador as far as the steps, having first begged him and all the others to return to the meeting-place at the appointed hour.

The End of the Fifth Night.

Night the Sixth.

Night the Sixth.

HE shadows of a night sombre and overcast had diffused themselves o'er all around, and the brilliant stars in the ample-domed heaven no longer gave their light, and Æolus, sweeping over the salt waves with a long-drawn moan, stirred up a tempestuous sea and blew hard against shipmen and voyagers, when our noble and faithful band of companions, caring nought for the violent wind or the swelling waves or for the cruel cold, betook themselves to their accustomed meeting-place and sat down in due order, having first made a respectful reverence to the Signora. She forthwith ordered the golden vase to be brought to her, and placed therein the names of five ladies. The first to be drawn out

was that of Alteria, the second of Arianna,
the third of Cateruzza, the fourth of
Lauretta, and the fifth of Eritrea. This
done the Signora directed these five to
sing a canzonetta, and they at once
obeyed her command and began to discourse sweetly the following song.

SONG.

O Love ! if faith rose with thee at thy birth ;
    If ye, twin flowers of earth,
    Should twine around my lady's name
    And deck the presence I adore ;
        Then never more
Should they divide, or time let sink my loyal flame.

She feels your power indeed, but not enough
    To let your onslaught rough
    Sway all her nature, and release
    Her passions kept so well in hand.
        And thus I stand
With failing hope, while my desire doth aye increase.

When the singing of this sweet and
most pleasant song was finished, Alteria,
who had been chosen to tell the first
story, laid aside her viol and bow and
thus began.

THE FIRST FABLE.

Two men who are close friends dupe one another and in the end have their wives in common.

ANY are the tricks and deceptions which men nowadays practise one upon another, but of the whole mass of these you will find none comparable in craft and knavery to those which one friend will use in imposing upon another. And since it has fallen to my lot to open the entertainment this evening with a story, it has come into my mind to give you an account of the subtlety and cunning and treachery which a certain man employed in the befooling of another who was a close friend of his own. And although the first one who tried this knavish game completely duped his friend by the amazing cunning he displayed, yet in the end he found himself tricked by a craft and ingenuity no whit inferior to his own. All of which shall be clearly set forth to you if you will of your kindness give a hearing to my story.

In the famous and ancient city of Genoa there lived in times past two friends, of whom one was called by name Messer Liberale Spinola, a man of great wealth, and at the same time one much addicted to the pleasures of the world, and the other Messer Arthilao Sara, one of the chief merchants of the city. The friendship between these two was very warm and close; so great, indeed, was their attachment the one for the other, that they could scarce endure to be apart. And if it should happen by any chance that either one of these had need of aught belonging to the other, he could claim it without delay or hindrance. And seeing that Messer Arthilao was engaged in numerous ventures in merchandise, and had in hand many affairs, both on his own account and on the account of others, he one day had to set out on a journey to Soria. Wherefore, having sought out his dear friend Messer Libe- .

rale, he thus addressed him in the same
sincere and benevolent spirit he ever felt
towards him : ' My friend, you know
well, and it is manifest to all men, how
great is the love and affection subsisting
between us, how I always have relied
and still rely upon you, both on account
of the friendship we have had for each
other for so many years past, and on
account of the vow of brotherhood that
there is between us. Wherefore, because
I have settled in my mind to go to Soria,
and because there is no other man in the
world whom I trust as I trust you, I
come with all boldness and confidence to
you to entreat you to do me a favour,
which thing, though it may cause no little disturbance to your own economy, I
beg that you of your goodness, and for
the sake of our mutual good feeling, will
not deny me.' Messer Liberale, who
was fully inclined to do his friend any
kindness he might ask for, without further words concerning the matter, said :
' Arthilao, my dear friend, the love we

have one for the other, and the bond of
fellowship which our sincere affection has
knitted between us, ought to render un-
necessary all such discourse as this. Tell
me now, without keeping aught behind,
what your wishes may be, and lay me
under your orders, for I am ready to discharge whatever duty you may put upon
me.' Then said Messer Arthilao to his
friend: 'My desire and request of you
is to beg you that, so long as I shall be
away, you will take under your charge
the government of my house, and in like
manner of my wife, calling her attention
to anything that may be wanted, and
whatever sum of money you may dis-
burse on her behalf I will pay you in
full on my return.' Messer Liberale,
when he understood what his friend
wanted of him, first gave him hearty
thanks for the high opinion he had of
his probity, in that he held him in such
good esteem,[1] then he freely promised
Messer Arthilao to discharge, to the best

[1] Orig., *del conto che facea.*

of his poor abilities, the task which had been put upon·him.

When the time had come for Messer Arthilao to set out on his voyage, having first bestowed all his merchandise on board his ship, he recommended his wife Daria — who, as it happened, was three months gone with child — to the care of his friend, and then set forth, sailing out of Genoa with his sails spread to a favouring wind, and with good fortune to aid him. As soon as Messer Arthilao was embarked and well on his way outward Messer Liberale betook himself to the house of Madonna Daria, his well-beloved neighbour, and thus spake to her: 'Madonna, Messer Arthilao, your good husband and my very dearest friend, before he set forth on this voyage, besought me with the most pressing entreaties to take under my charge the care of all his affairs, and of you yourself, madonna, as well; and likewise to keep you mindful of all the things for your good of which you may stand in

need. I, for the sake of the affection
which always has existed and still exists
between him and me, promised him that
I would perform any duty he might lay
upon me. Wherefore I have come to
you at once in order that you may let
me know your will, without hindrance,
concerning any matter which may suggest itself to you.'

Now Madonna Daria, who was by
nature very sweet and gentle, thanked
Messer Liberale heartily for this speech,
begging him at the same time to be as
good as his word if at any time she
should find herself in need of his good
offices. To this Messer Liberale answered that he assuredly would not fail
her, and, in discharge of his promise, he
was very constant in his visits to his fair
neighbour, and took good care that she
wanted for nothing. In the course of
time it came to his knowledge that she
was with child, but feigning to be ignorant thereof, he said one day to her,
'Madonna, how are you feeling? doubt-

less somewhat estranged on account of
the absence of your husband, Messer
Arthilao.' And to this Madonna Daria
answered, 'Of a surety, my good neighbour, I feel his absence for many reasons, but above all on account of my
present condition.' 'And in what condition,' said Messer Liberale, 'may you
find yourself?' 'I am three months
gone with child,' Madonna Daria replied, 'and there is moreover something
strange about this pregnancy of mine.
I never felt myself so ill at ease before.'
Messer Liberale when he heard this said,
'But, my good neighbour, are you really
with child?' 'I would it were you instead, my friend,' said Madonna Daria,
'and that I were well quit of it.'[1]

Now on account of what had passed
it ensued that, in the course of inter-
views of this kind with his fair neighbour, Messer Liberale was so much
charmed by her beauty and her soft
plump figure, that he became hotly in-

[1] Orig., *e io farei digiuna.*

flamed with amorous desire for her, and
night and day could turn his thoughts
to nothing else than how he might obtain gratification of his dishonest wishes,
but the love in which he held his friend
Messer Arthilao kept him back for a
time. But after a while, spurred on
by the violence of his passion, which
melted all his good resolutions, he went
one day to Madonna Daria, and said,
'Alas! my dear friend, how deeply
grieved I am that Messer Arthilao
should thus have gone away from you
and left you pregnant; because, on account of his sudden departure, he may
very well have forgotten to complete
the child which he begat and which you
now carry in your womb. On this account, perchance, it has come to pass that
your pregnancy is such an uneasy one.'
'O! my friend,' cried Madonna Daria,
'do you really believe that the infant
which I bear in my womb may be lacking in one or other of its limbs, and
that I may be suffering therefor?' 'Of

a truth,' replied Messer Liberale, 'that is my opinion; nay, I hold it for certain that my good friend Messer Arthilao failed to give it the due number of limbs. It often happens in cases of this sort that one child is born lame and another blind, one of this fashion and another of that.' 'Ah! my dear friend,' said Madonna Daria, 'this thing you tell me greatly troubles my mind. Where shall I look for a remedy, so that this misfortune may not befall me?' 'My dear neighbour,' Messer Liberale replied, 'be of good cheer and do not distress yourself in vain, for know that a remedy is to be found for everything except death.' 'I beg you, for the love you bear to your absent friend,' said Madonna Daria, 'that you will put me in the way of finding this remedy; and the sooner you can let me have it, the more I shall be bound to you; then there will be no danger lest the child should be born imperfect.

When Messer Liberale found that he

had brought Madonna Daria into a mood favourable for his purpose, he said to her: ' Dear lady, it would be great baseness and cowardice in a man if, when he saw his friend ready to perish, he did not stretch out his hand to aid him. Wherefore, seeing that I am able to supply the defects which your infant at present has, I should be a traitor to you and should be working you great wrong if I did not come to your assistance.' ' Then, my dear friend,' said the lady, ' do not make any longer delay, but set to work straightway, so that the child may be made perfect at once; for, besides the pity of it, it would be a most grievous sin.' ' Do not let any doubt on this score trouble you,' said Liberale; ' I will discharge my duty to the full; and now give orders to your waiting-woman that she get ready the table, and in the mean time we will make a beginning of the good work we have in hand.'

Thus, while the waiting-woman was

getting in order the table, Messer Liberale went with Madonna Daria into the bedchamber, and having made fast the door, he began to caress her and kiss her, giving her the most loving embracements man ever gave to woman. Madonna Daria was mightily astonished when she saw what Messer Liberale's treatment was, and said to him; 'What does this mean, Messer Liberale? Is it right that we should do such things in such fashion, good neighbours and friends though we be? Alack a day! it is too great a sin; though, if this were not so, I do not know that I should refuse to consent to your wishes.'

Then replied Messer Liberale, 'Pray tell me which is the greater sin, to lie with your friend, or to let this infant come into the world maimed and imperfect?' 'I judge that the greater sin would be,' replied Madonna Daria, 'to let a child be born, through the fault of its parents, in an imperfect state.' 'Then,' rejoined Messer Liberale, 'you

would assuredly be guilty of a great
offence were you to refuse to let me
bring to pass all that work your husband left undone in the formation of
the child.' Now the lady, who desired
greatly that her offspring should come
into the world perfect in all its members,
gave credence to these words of her
neighbour, and, notwithstanding the close
tie between him and her husband, she
gave way to his desires, and many and
many a time hereafter they took their
pleasure together. Indeed, so pleasant
to the lady seemed this method of restoring to her infant whatever might
be wanting, that she was ever begging
Messer Liberale to take good heed lest
he should fail, as her husband had failed
before. Liberale, who found he had
fallen upon a very dainty morsel, did his
best, both by day and night, to make up
anything which might be wanting in the
child, so that it might be born perfect
in every way. And when Madonna
Daria had gone her full time, she was

brought to bed with a lusty boy, who
proved to be the very counterpart of
Messer Arthilao, and perfectly formed,
lacking nothing whatsoever in any of his
parts. On this score the lady was over-
joyed, and full of gratitude to Messer
Liberale as the cause of her good fortune.

After a short time had passed Messer
Arthilao returned to Genoa and betook
himself to his home, where he found
his wife restored to health and fair as
ever, and she, full of joy and merriment, ran to meet him with her baby
in her arms, and they embraced and
kissed one another heartily. And as
soon as Messer Liberale got news of
the return of his friend, he quickly
went to see and greet him, congratulat-
ing him on his happy return and on
his well-being. A few weeks later it
happened that Messer Arthilao, as he
sat at table one day with his wife and
fondled the child, spake thus: 'O
Daria, my wife, what a beautiful child

this one of ours is!   Did you ever see
one better made?   Look at its whole
presence, and admire its pretty face and
its bright eyes, which sparkle as if they
were stars!'   And thus, feature by feature, he went on praising the shapely
boy.   Then Madonna Daria answered :
'Of a truth there is nothing wanting in
him, but that is not altogether owing to
your fine performances, my good man ;
because, as you know well enough, I
was three months gone with child when
you went away, and the child which I
had conceived was not yet fully furnished with his members, whereby I
had like to have had grave mischance
in my pregnancy.   Wherefore we have
great cause to thank our good neighbour Messer Liberale, who was most
eager and diligent to supply out of his
own strength all that was lacking in
the child, making good all those parts
where your own work had failed.'
Messer Arthilao listened to and fully
understood this speech of his wife, and

felt wellnigh beside himself with rage. It seemed as if he had a sharp knife in his heart, for he quickly comprehended that Messer Liberale had played the traitor to him and had debauched his wife; but, like a sensible man, he feigned not to have understood the meaning of what he had heard, and held his peace, turning the discourse, when he spoke again, upon other matters.

But when he was risen from the table, Messer Arthilao began to cogitate over the strange and shameful conduct of his friend, whom he had loved and esteemed far above any other man in the world, and day and night he brooded and planned in what fashion, and by what method, he might best avenge himself for the great offence which had been wrought against his honour. The poor wight, thus enraged, harboured ever these projects, scarcely knowing what course he would take, but in the end he determined to

do a certain thing which would let him
bring to pass the issue he especially
willed and desired. Wherefore one day
he said to his wife, ' Daria, see that to-
morrow our table may be furnished a
little more generously than is our wont,
because I wish to invite Messer Liberale
and Madonna Propertia his wife, our
good neighbours, to dine with us ; but
take heed that, as you love your life, you
speak not a word of any sort, and let pass
anything you may see or hear without re-
mark or notice.' And Madonna Daria
agreed to do as he proposed. Then having left the house he betook himself to
the piazza, where he met his neighbour,
Messer Liberale, whom, together with
his wife, Madonna Propertia, he bade
come together on the following day.
And Messer Liberale gladly accepted
the invitation.

On the following day the two invited
guests repaired to the house of Messer
Arthilao, where they met a most friendly
greeting and reception. And when they

were all gathered together and were conversing on this thing and that, Messer Arthilao spake thus to Madonna Propertia : ' Dear neighbour, while they are getting ready the viands and setting the table, I would you took some trifle to sustain you.' And, having led her aside into a chamber, he handed to her a beaker of drugged wine with a toast thereto, both of which she took, and, without any fear whatever, ate the toast and emptied the beaker of wine. Then they returned, and, having placed themselves at the table, began merrily the dinner.

. But long before the feast had come to an end, Madonna Propertia began to feel drowsiness stealing over her, so that she could scarce hold open her eyes, and Messer Arthilao when he perceived this said : ' Madonna, will it please you to go and rest yourself a little ; peradventure last night your slumber was broken,' and with these words he conducted her into a chamber where, having thrown herself upon the bed, she fell asleep at

once. Messer Arthilao, fearing lest the
potency of his draught should pass off,[1]
and that time might fail him for the carrying out of the project which he was
secretly keeping in his mind, called Messer Liberale and said to ·him : ' Neighbour, let us go out for a little, and leave
your good wife to sleep as long as she
may need; peradventure she was astir
somewhat too early this morning and is.
in want of sleep.'   Then they both went
out and betook themselves to the piazza,
where Messer Arthilao made believe to
be pressed in the despatch of certain matters of business, and having bidden farewell to his friend, returned privily to his
own house, and, being come there, stole
quietly into the chamber where Madonna
Propertia was lying.   When he went up
to the bed he perceived that she was
sleeping quietly, whereupon, without being espied by any one of the people in ·
the house or rousing the notice of the
lady herself, he took away from her, with

[1] Orig., *non venisse à meno.*

the utmost lightness of hand, the rings she wore on her fingers and the pearls from about her neck, and withdrew from the chamber.

The effects of the medicated draught had entirely dissipated themselves by the time Madonna Propertia awoke, and, when she felt inclined to rise and leave the bed, she remarked that her pearls and her rings were missing; so, having got up, she searched here and there and everywhere, turning everything upside down without finding any trace of the thing she was seeking. Wherefore, mightily upset, she rushed out of the room and began to question Madonna Daria whether by chance she might not have taken her pearls and rings, but Madonna Daria assured her friend that she had seen nothing of them; whereupon Madonna Propertia was wellnigh beside herself with agony. While the poor lady was thus distraught with grief and anxiety, without any notion as to where she should seek a remedy for her trouble, who should come in but Messer Arthilao, and he, when he saw his friend's wife so painfully agitated, said in a somewhat diffident tone: 'What has come to you, dear friend, that you are in such trouble?' In answer to this question Madonna Propertia told him the whole misfortune which had befallen her; whereupon Messer Arthilao, making as if he knew nought of the matter, thus spake to her: 'Make a close search, Madonna, and consider well whether you may not have put these your jewels in some place which you no longer remember. But in any case, supposing that you should not be able to find them, I promise you, on the faith of our old friendship, that I will make such an investigation of the matter that they who have taken away these things of yours will find they have played a bad turn for themselves; but first, before we put our hands to the business, I beg that you will once more make a diligent search in every corner.

Whereupon the ladies and the serving-women as well searched and re-searched the house from top to bottom, turning everything upside down and finding nothing. Messer Arthilao remarking their ill success, began to make an uproar through the house, threatening now this one and now that with ill handling, but they all swore solemnly that they had no knowledge of the matter. Then Messer Arthilao, turning towards Madonna Propertia said : 'My dear neighbour, be not overcome by this trouble, but keep a light heart, for I am at your service to see this matter to an end. And you must know, my dear friend, that I am the possessor of a secret of so great virtue and efficiency that by its working I shall be able to lay my hand on the man, whoever he may be, who has taken your jewels.

When she heard these words Madonna Propertia said : 'Oh, Messer Arthilao ! of your kindness I beg you to make this experiment, in order that there may

be no cause for Messer Liberale to sus-
pect me, or to think of me as an evil-
doer.'   Whereupon Messer Arthilao,
seeing that the time was now come when
he might meetly work his vengeance for
the injury which had been done him of
late, called for his wife and for the serving-women, and strictly charged them
that they should get them gone out of
the chamber, and that no one of them
should dare to come near to it under
any pretence, except he should summon
her thither.   And when his wife and the
women folk were gone, Messer Arthilao
closed the door of the chamber, and
having drawn with a bit of charcoal a
circle on the floor and figured therein
certain signs and characters of his own
invention, said to Madonna Propertia:
' Now, my dear friend, lie down on that
bed and take heed you move not, neither
have any fear on account of anything
you may feel, forasmuch as I will not
go hence till I shall have found your
jewels.'   ' You need not have the small-

est fear,' said Madonna Propertia, 'that I will budge an inch, nor indeed do the least thing of any sort, unless I have your commands thereanent.' Then Messer Arthilao, having turned himself towards the right, made certain signs upon the floor, then turning to the left made other signs and conjurations in the air, and pretending the while to be conversing with a multitude of spirits, uttered all sorts of strange noises in a fictitious voice in such a way that Madonna Propertia was not a little bewildered, but Messer Arthilao, who had foreseen this, reassured her, and speaking comforting words to her bade her not to be affrighted. And when he had been within the circle for about half a quarter of an hour, he began to speak certain words in a gurgling tone, which were as follows :

What I have not found, what I am seeking still,
Lies hid in a valley deep beneath a smiling hill;
The one who holds it now, is the one who lost it
    then ;
So take your fishing-rod and you'll win it back again.

Madonna Propertia was fully as much
astonished as pleased as she listened to
these words, and, when the incantation
was finished, Messer Arthilao said:
'Dear friend, you have heard all that
was said. The jewels which, as you believed, you have lost, are somewhere
about you. There is no need for any
further grief. Keep up your spirits, and
we will find them all. But it is necessary that I should seek for them in the
place where you understand they are.'
The lady, who was very desirous to get
back her jewels, answered eagerly: 'Good
friend, I fully comprehend all this. Do
not delay, I beg you, but begin your
search with all despatch.' Whereupon
Messer Arthilao came forth out of the
circle, and, having made ready for his
sport by lying down beside the lady on
the bed, straightway began his fishing,
and at the same moment when he made
his first cast, he drew forth a ring from
his bosom (without the lady seeing it),
and this he handed to her, saying: 'See,

Madonna, how successful, how good a
fisherman I am, how at the first cast I
have recovered your diamond!' Madonna Propertia, when she saw the diamond, was greatly pleased and said:
'Ah, my good, kind friend! I pray you
not yet to cease your fishing; then perhaps you will get back all the other jewels I have lost.' Messer Arthilao kept
on at his angling like a man, now bringing out one lost jewel, now another,
working so well with his tackle that
finally he recovered and handed back to
the lady every article that had been lost.

For this service Madonna Propertia
was highly grateful and quite satisfied
with the issue of the affair, and, having
got back all her precious jewels, she said
to Messer Arthilao: ' Dear friend, see
how many and valuable things you have
recovered for me by your good faith and
diligence; peradventure by another cast
of your line in the same place you might
win back for me a beautiful little kettle
which was stolen from me some days

ago and which I prized very highly.'
Then Messer Arthilao answered : ' Most
willingly would I do this, were I not
somewhat wearied just at present over
what I have already done. Be assured
that at some future time I shall be quite
ready to make a trial to get back your
kettle, and I have good hope that we
may succeed.' Madonna Propertia was
fully content with this proposition, and,
having taken leave of Messer Arthilao
and Donna Daria, she took her jewels
and returned home with a light heart.

A short time after this it happened
that one morning, when Madonna Propertia was lying in bed with her husband,
and the two chatting pleasantly together,
she said to him : ' Oh, husband ! i'faith
consider whether you might not, by taking a turn of fishing, find for me the little kettle which we lost a long time ago ;
because, forsooth, some days since I happened to miss certain of my jewels, and
Messer Arthilao, our good neighbour,
was kind enough to come to my aid,

and, by fishing for them most skilfully, found every one of them and gave them back to me. And when I begged him that he would try another cast with the view of finding the kettle, he told me that he was unable to recover it just then, seeing that he had wearied himself somewhat by the fishing he had already done on my behalf. Wherefore, I beg you, let us two make a trial to see whether we may not be able to get it back.'

Messer Liberale, when he listened to this speech, understood well enough what manner of repayment his neighbour had made him for his own trick, and, holding his peace, was fain to pocket the affront patiently. On the following morning the two neighbours, when they met upon the piazza, looked narrowly one at the other, but neither of them had the courage to broach the subject, so nothing was said on one side or the other. Nor did they take their wives into their confidence, but the issue of the affair was that for the future a common right was established for either one to take his diversion with the wife of the other.

This story told by Alteria was so mightily to the taste of the company that it seemed as if they would have gone on for the rest of the evening making remarks thereanent, and discussing the craft and dexterity with which the one friend had duped the other. But the Signora, when she saw that the laughter and the frolicsome speeches promised to go on somewhat longer than was meet, gave the word that the merriment should stop, and that Alteria should follow the established rule by propounding her enigma. Whereupon she, without making any further delay, thus gave it:

A useful thing, firm, hard, and white,
Outside in shaggy robe bedight;
Hollowed within right cleverly,
It goes to work both white and dry.
When after labour it comes back,
You'll find it moist and very black;

For service it is ready ever,
And fails the hand that guides it never.

This enigma given by Alteria awakened amongst her hearers fully as much pleasure as had her story. And, notwithstanding the fact that certain traits thereof might seem somewhat to affront modesty, the ladies did not on this account forbear to discuss it, because they had on another occasion heard the same thing. But Lauretta, feigning to have no inkling of the meaning of the enigma, besought Alteria to explain it, and the latter, with a merry countenance, spake thus to her questioner: " It is superfluous labour to carry crocodiles to Egypt, or vases to Samos, or owls to Athens. However, to do your pleasure, I will unfold my riddle. I declare that the instrument, partly plumed and partly perforated, is simply a pen such as one employs in writing, which, before one dips it in the inkstand, is white and dry, but when it is withdrawn therefrom

is black and moistened and ready to
serve the writer who holds it in whatever way he will."   As soon as Alteria
had finished this explanation of her pretty riddle, Arianna, who was sitting beside
her, stood up and began to tell her story.

THE SECOND FABLE.

Castorio, wishing to become fat, submits himself
to treatment at the hands of Sandro, and being
half dead thereby is soothed by a jest of Sandro's wife.

THE fable which Alteria has just
told to us with no less grace
than discretion calls back to
my mind a certain drollery, as
laughable perchance as hers, which I
heard briefly told from the mouth of a
noble gentlewoman a short time agone.
And, if I should not succeed in setting
it forth with that distinction and elegance
with which it was told to me, I must
beg you to hold me excused, seeing that
nature has been niggard to me of those

fine qualities granted so liberally to the lady of whom I speak.

Somewhat below Fano, a city of the Marches, situated on the shore of the Adriatic sea, there is a small town called Carignano, numbering amongst its people many lusty youths and fair damsels, and there, amongst others, dwelt a peasant named Sandro, one of the most witty and rollicking fellows nature ever made, and, for the reason that he recked nought of anything save what gave him pleasure, let things go well or ill, he became so ruddy and fat that his flesh resembled nothing so much as a bit of larded bacon. And he, when he had come to the age of forty, took to wife a woman just as good-humoured and fat as himself, and a week never passed in which this good woman would not carefully shave her husband's beard in order that he might look more seemly and frolicsome. It chanced that a certain Messer Castorio, a gentleman of Fano, rich and young, but of slender wit, purchased in the com-

mune of Carignano a farm, on which
stood a house of moderate size, and
there, with two of his servants and a lady
whom he entertained for his pleasure, he
would spend a greater part of the summer.   One day when Castorio, according to his custom, was walking through
the fields after dinner, he marked Sandro, who was turning up the earth with
his crooked plough, and seeing what a
fine fat ruddy fellow the peasant was
with his smiling face, he said: 'Good
neighbour, I cannot think what can be
the reason that I am so lank and lean,
as you see, while you are ruddy and well
fleshed.   Every day I eat the nicest
viands and drink the costliest wines; I
lie in bed as long as pleases me, and want
for nothing.   No man in all the world
longs so keenly as I do to get fat, but
the greater pains I take to that end, the
leaner I grow.   Now all the winter you
eat nought but the coarsest food, and
drink watered wine; you rise up to go
to your work while it is yet night, and

all summer long you never have an
hour's rest; nevertheless your rosy face
and your well-covered ribs make you a
pleasure to behold. Wherefore, being
greatly desirous to become fat, I beg you
that you will, to the best of your knowledge and power, help me to lay on flesh,
and tell me the method you have employed so greatly to your own advantage.
Then, over and beyond the fifty gold
florins which I purpose to give you forthwith, I promise to reward you in such
wise that, for the rest of your life, you
will assuredly be well satisfied with what
I do for you, and rest content.'

Now Sandro, who was both cunning
and roguish in grain, and was one of the
red-haired sort, refused flatly to tell Castorio what he wanted to know so eagerly; but, after a little, feigning to be
overcome by the importunities of Castorio, and amazingly taken in reality by
the notion of fingering those fifty gold
florins, he let loose his tongue somewhat,
and, having given over his ploughing

for a little, he sat down beside Castorio and spake thus: 'Signor Castorio, you say you are mightily astonished over my fatness and likewise over your own lean condition, believing the while that a man gets fat or thin by reason of what he may eat or drink; but in this you are vastly in error, for one may see any day eaters in any number, and drinkers as well, who rather gormandize than eat their food, and nevertheless are as thin as lizards.   But if you will do for yourself what I have done, I will warrant you will soon be as fat as I am.'   Then said Castorio, 'And what is the thing you did?' Sandro answered, 'Why, about a year ago I made a gelding of myself, and from the self-same hour when I did this I grew fat as you see.' 'But I wonder you did not meet your death thereby,' replied Castorio. 'What do you mean by death?' cried Sandro, 'seeing that the practitioner who did the business for me had such skill of hand that I felt not the least pain or hurt, and

from that very time my flesh has been
like the flesh of a young child. Of a
truth I have never felt myself so well
and happy as I find myself to-day.' 'And
tell me, I pray you, the name of the man
who did this service to you,' said Cas-
toria. 'Ah! but he is dead, good man,'
replied Sandro. 'Alas! cried Castorio,
'what shall we do then seeing that he is
dead?' Then Sandro answered : 'Do
not be cast down; let me tell you that
this good man, before he gave up the
ghost, taught me, and made me the
master of his art, which, from that time
onward, I have regularly practised, cas-
trating vast quantities of calves and fowls
and other animals, which, as soon as I
have tried my hand upon them, always
lay on fat in a fashion that is wonderful
to behold. Now, if you will only leave
the charge of this matter to me, I will
pledge myself that you will be highly
contented with my handiwork.' 'But
I fear I may die under the operation,'
said Castorio. 'What folly is this you

say? Death, forsooth! Look at the
calves and the capons and the other
animals I deal with in my calling;
how many of these die?' cried Sandro.
Whereupon Castorio, who was possessed
with a stronger desire to grow fat than
had ever infected man before, said he
would take time to consider the business.

But Sandro, who saw that Castorio in
truth was fully determined to follow the
advice he had given him, bade him not
delay, but to allow him straightway to
try his art upon him.   The foolish fellow agreed, and Sandro, who had with
him a knife as sharp as a razor, at once
set to work, and in a few seconds of time
made a capon of Messer Castorio.   Then
he took some sweet oil and the juice of
certain herbs and made therewith a dressing, which he applied to the wound, and
then helped Castorio to get up on his
feet, as proper a eunuch as there was in
the world.   Castorio put his hand in his
pocket and took therefrom fifty golden

florins, which he gave to Sandro, and then, having taken leave of the crafty peasant, he went back to his house.

But before Castorio had known an hour's experience of life as a gelding, he began to feel the greatest pain and anguish that ever man had felt. He could never get rest for a single moment, and day by day his trouble increased, so that he was in great danger of death, and at the same time an offence to those about him. When this intelligence came to Sandro's ears, he was mightily affrighted thereanent, and began heartily to wish that he had never played this scurvy trick upon Castorio, fearing lest the latter should indeed die of his injuries. Castorio, when he found himself brought into such a pitiable state, was so inflamed with rage on account of the pain he suffered and of the disgrace which must fall upon him, that he determined at all hazard to kill Sandro forthwith. So, to set about the business in the fashion he judged most fitting, he went, accom-

panied by two of his servants, to the
house of Sandro, whom he found at supper, and spake thus: ' Sandro, this is a
fine trick you have played me, and one
which will assuredly be the death of me;
but before I die I promise you shall pay
the price of the wickedness you have
wrought.'   To this Sandro replied:
' The affair was your own and none of
mine, because it was by your prayers
and supplications alone that I was induced to do this thing for you.   But,
in order that I may not seem to you as
wanting in skill over my work, nor ungrateful for the reward you have given
me, nor be reckoned as the cause of
your undoing, I will ask you to come
to me to-morrow morning in good time
in my field, and there I will give you
relief which will set you free at once
from all fear of death on account of your
ailment.'

As soon as Castorio had gone Sandro
broke out into bitter weeping, wishing
anxiously to fly the country at once and

to betake himself into some foreign land,
deeming that he heard the tread of
the officer of justice always at his heels,
about to put him in bonds. His wife,
when she saw how overwrought with
grief and care he was, and knowing
nought of the reason thereof, inquired
of him why he bore himself thus mourn-
fully, whereupon he told her the whole
story, word for word. The wife, as
soon as she had rightly comprehended
the cause of her husband's dismay, and
taken heed, moreover, of the fact that
Castorio himself was a dolt and a wit-
ling, and that he of a surety stood in
some peril of death, was at first somewhat troubled in mind herself, and began by rating her husband for his folly
in thus having thrust his head into such
danger. But afterwards she fell into a
gentler mood, and comforted him, begging him to keep a light heart, for she
would set to work to order the course
of events so that he would be free from
all serious danger.

Next morning, when the appointed
hour had come, the wife took the garments of Sandro her husband, and,
having put them on her back and a cap
upon her head, she went afield with the
oxen and the plough and set to work
to plough the land, keeping a watch to
see whether Castorio came as appointed
or not.   Before long he appeared, and,
deeming that the wife of Sandro must
be Sandro himself at work ploughing
his field, he spake thus: "Sandrin,[1] je
meurs si ne prens pitié de moy, car la
playe que m'as faicte n'est encores refermée, joint que la chair en est toute
pourrie, et rend telle puanteur que je
doubte de mon salut.   Et si en bref
ne me donnes le remède nécessaire, tu
me verras mourir à les pieds.'   La
femme desguisée en Sandrin luy de-
manda veoir sa playe, et qu'elle y pour-
voiroit.   Adonc Castor, destachant sa
brayette et hausante le devant de sa
chemise, luy monstra l'overture que le

[1] Translation by Pierre de la Rivey.

chancre avoit desja toute gastée. Ce
que voiant, ceste femme luy dit en souz-
riant : ' Monsieur, vous monstrez bien
que n'avez point de cœur de craindre la
mort pour si peu de chose, que pensez
neantmoins irreparable ; mais vous estes
trompé si le croyez ainsi ; et quoy ! si
vous estiez comme moy, que seroit ce ?
Il y a un an entier que ma playe me fut
faicte beaucoup plus grand que la vostre, toutesfois elle n'est encores consoli-
dée, neantmoins vous voyez comme je
suis gras, potelé et frais comme un
œillet. Et affin que ne doutiez de ce
que je vous dy, je vous en veux bien
monstrer l'expérience.' Ce disant, s'af-
fermit d'une jambe contre terre, et levant l'autre sur les manches de la
charue, haussa ses accoustrements et
laschant une vesse lui fit baisser la teste
pour regarder. Castor voyant ceste
grand overture, n'estre encor refermée
depuis le temps, se rejouist en soy
meme, deliberant de là en avant en-
durer patiemment la douleur que pro-

venoit de ceste incisure.   Tellement
que prenant courage au bout de quelque
temps le pauvret commenca a se guarir
et devenir si gras et refaict qu'il don-
noit plaisir a qui le regardoit.

Les dames risent assez de Castro lequel estoit demeuré sans tesmoings mais
la risée des hommes fut beaucoup plus
grande quand ils veirent la femme de
Sandrin, desguisée en son mary, lui
monstra la nature.   Et pour ce qu'au-
cun de la troupe ne se pouvoit abstenir
de rire Madame se frappant les mains
l'une contre l'autre fit signe qu'on se
teust et qu'Ariane suivist l'ordre en
recitant son enigme.   La quelle pour
ne sembler moins propre et gentille que
les autres, dit ainsi :

Je veux que mon amy sur le ventre se couche,
Et pour le soulager voici ce que je fais ;
Je prens a belles mains la chose, et puis la mets
Dedans le trou ouvert si bien que je le bouche.
Après en l'œilladant d'un regard comme louche,
Poussant et repoussant sans jamais avoir paix.
Je laisse cheoir dedans je ne scay quoy d'epais,

Dont le tiede degout le rend morne et farouche.
Il se plaint sur la fin ; mais, pour l'encourager,
Et les tristes pensers de son cœur estranger,
Toujours je l'entretiens de toute ma puissance,
Tellement que jamais il n'est de moi laissé,
Que l'un, tout estonné, n'en ait pleine la pance,
Et l'outre ne s'en aille et recrue et lassé.

L'enigme raconté par Ariane blessa un peu les aureilles des auditeurs lesquels le trouvèrent aucunement vergongeux. Au moyen de quoy Madame, la reprenant avec aigres paroles, luy monstra qu'elle n'en estoit contente. Mais la gentile demoiselle, qui estoit toute plaisante et gaillarde, d'un visage ouvert et joyaux s'excusa disant : 'Soubs vostre reverence, Madame, vous n'avez juste occasion vous fascher à l'encontre de moy d'autant que mon enigme qui porte seulement avec soy un ridicule effect n'est deshonneste comme on le pense, et voicy la raison : Quand on veut bailler un clystère à un malade, ne le faict on pas plus souvent coucher sur le ventre ? Après, ne prend on pas à

belles mains la chose, c'est a dire la
seringue, et la met on pas dans le trou?
Et pour ce que le malade prend le clystère contre son gré, se plaignant ordi-
nairement, ne luy dict on pas qu'il ne
se fasche, ains prenne courage? D'a-
vantage celle qui luy donne, en poussant
et repoussant, ne luy emplit elle pas la
pance de la decoction? Ce faicte s'en
retourne elle pas quasi toute lasse de la
peine qu'elle a prise à l'entour du malade? Ainsi voyez vous, noble assis-
tence, mon enigme n'estre tant sale et
vicieux que le faisiez du commence-
ment."

The Signora, as soon as she heard
and understood this excellent interpretation of the laughable riddle, was ap-
peased, and gave leave henceforth to
the story-tellers to say whatsoever they
would, without fear of being called to
account. Cateruzza, whose turn it was
to tell the third story, perceiving that
the Signora's anger was moderated, and
that free field had been given to her for

her discourse, began her story in an animated style as follows.

THE THIRD FABLE.

𝕻𝖔𝖑𝖎𝖘𝖘𝖊𝖓𝖆, 𝖆 𝖜𝖎𝖉𝖔𝖜, 𝖍𝖆𝖘 𝖉𝖎𝖇𝖊𝖗𝖘 𝖑𝖔𝖇𝖊𝖗𝖘. 𝕻𝖆𝖓𝖙𝖆𝖑𝖎𝖔, 𝖍𝖊𝖗 𝖘𝖔𝖓, 𝖗𝖊𝖕𝖗𝖔𝖇𝖊𝖘 𝖍𝖊𝖗 𝖙𝖍𝖊𝖗𝖊𝖆𝖓𝖊𝖓𝖙, 𝖜𝖍𝖊𝖗𝖊𝖚𝖕𝖔𝖓 𝖘𝖍𝖊 𝖕𝖗𝖔𝖒𝖎𝖘𝖊𝖘 𝖙𝖔 𝖒𝖊𝖓𝖉 𝖍𝖊𝖗 𝖜𝖆𝖞𝖘 𝖎𝖋 𝖍𝖊 𝖜𝖎𝖑𝖑 𝖑𝖆𝖞 𝖆𝖘𝖎𝖉𝖊 𝖈𝖊𝖗𝖙𝖆𝖎𝖓 𝖚𝖓𝖈𝖔𝖚𝖙𝖍 𝖍𝖆𝖇𝖎𝖙𝖘. 𝕳𝖊 𝖆𝖌𝖗𝖊𝖊𝖘, 𝖇𝖚𝖙 𝖍𝖎𝖘 𝖒𝖔𝖙𝖍𝖊𝖗 𝖉𝖚𝖕𝖊𝖘 𝖍𝖎𝖒, 𝖆𝖓𝖉 𝖋𝖎𝖓𝖆𝖑𝖑𝖞 𝖙𝖍𝖊𝖞 𝖌𝖔 𝖔𝖓 𝖎𝖓 𝖙𝖍𝖊𝖎𝖗 𝖔𝖑𝖉 𝖈𝖔𝖚𝖗𝖘𝖊𝖘.

A WOMAN, when once she becomes thoroughly wedded to a certain practice, whether it be good or bad, finds it a hard matter to abstain therefrom, seeing that she is by nature disposed to continue to the end of her days in whatever habits she may have adopted. Wherefore I now purpose to tell you a story of an adventure which happened to a young widow, who, having lived a wanton's life a long time, could not by any means break away from it. Nay, even when her own son, moved by righteous desire, lovingly reproved her,

she played a wily trick upon him in her
subtle treachery, and went on in her evil
ways.   All of this I will set forth fully
in the course of my tale.

There once lived, gracious ladies (it
was not long ago, and on that account
you may peradventure know something
thereof), in the splendid and renowned
city of Venice, a pretty little widow,
who was called by name Polissena, still
young in years and exceeding beautiful
in person, but of very low estate. This
woman had brought forth by her husband, who was dead, a son named Panfilio, a youth of good parts, of virtuous
life, and of praiseworthy manners, who
was at this time a goldsmith by trade.
And because (as I have already said)
Polissena was young, very handsome,
and graceful, many gallants — and
amongst these were some of the chief-
est nobles of the city — cast amorous
eyes upon her and wooed her persistently.
And she, who in former days had tasted
freely of the pleasures of the world and

of the sweetness of love's commerce, was not slow in giving assent to the solicitations of her wooers, and delivered herself up, body and soul, to the embraces of all those who would have her. So hot and amorous was her temper that she did not confine herself to the endearments of one or two lovers (which, seeing that she was young and so early left a widow, would have been a pardonable fault), but granted the favour of her person to all comers, having no regard for her own honour or for the honour of her husband.

Panfilio, who was fully cognizant of his mother's way of life (not that he in any way favoured it, but because from time to time he could not escape witnessing her shameful carriage), was deeply grieved thereanent, and suffered the deepest anguish of heart and that mental suffering, so hard to be borne, which any man of upright mind would of necessity feel in such a pass. Wherefore the wretched youth, living from

day to day with his soul vexed by these
torments, and not seldom feeling that
the burden of his disgrace was more
than he could endure, would ofttimes
take council with himself whether it
would not be better for him to slay his
mother outright; but when he remem-
bered that he had taken his being from
her, he let go this cruel purpose and
resolved to see whether he might not
prevail upon her by words, and induce
her to adopt a more cleanly manner of
life. So one day he seized an oppor-
tune moment, and, having seated himself beside his mother, addressed her
affectionately in the following terms:
' My beloved and honoured mother, it
is with the greatest grief and distress
that I now venture to approach you,
and I am sure you will not refuse to
lend your ears and listen to what I have
to say. It is something which I have,
until now, kept close hidden in my own
heart. Formerly I believed you to be
wise, prudent, and circumspect; but

now, to my sorrow, I know too well
that you are none of these things, and
so grieved am I on this account that I
would to God I were as far from you as
I am near you.[1] You, as far as I can
understand, are given over to the most
scandalous life, one which alike stains
your own honour and the good name
of my late father, your husband. And
if you will not have any regard for your
own character, I beg you at least to
show some consideration for me, seeing
that I am your only son, and one in
whom you may reckon to find a firm
and faithful support of your old age.'

The mother, when she had listened
to these words of her son, laughed in
his face and went on with her shameful
manner of life as before. Panfilio, perceiving that she was in nowise moved by
his entreaties and kindly words, resolved
to waste his breath no more, but to let
her go on as she list. It chanced that
not many days after this, Panfilio, by a

---

[1] Orig., *esser tanto da lungi, quanto io vi sono da presso.*

stroke of ill fortune, became infected
with the itch, and in so malignant a form
that he could scarce have fared worse had
he been a leper. Besides, the weather
was at this time very cold, and on this
account he found it impossible to get
cured of his distemper. In the evening
poor Panfilio would sit anear the fire,
and the heat thereof, inflaming his blood
all the more, aggravated the itch tenfold
and caused him to scratch himself without ceasing and to work himself into a
frenzy. One evening, as he sat before
the fire, as was his wont, scratching himself, there came to the house one of his
mother's lovers, and tarried a long time
with her in amorous conversation. The
wretched youth, besides being annoyed
by the irritating scabs which vexed him
cruelly, was further tormented and
pierced to the heart at the sight of his
mother in dalliance with her paramour.
When at last the latter had taken his
leave, Panfilio (still scratching his scabs)
said to his mother : ' Mother, some time

ago I exhorted you to restrain your lust and abandon this evil and dishonest manner of life, which covers you with foul shame and brings to me, who am your son, no small injury and ill-fame. But you, like the wanton woman you are, turned a deaf ear to what I had to say, and preferred to go on in the guilty indulgence of your carnal appetites rather than listen to my counsel Ah, my dear mother! I entreat you to have done with this disgraceful way of living. Keep that honour, which it is your duty to preserve, and cast this shame from you, and do not seek to kill me with grief and ill-fame. Do you not see that you may, at any moment, be called to your account, inasmuch as death is always by our side? Do you not hear what evil things are said of you at every corner?'

While Panfilio was giving forth this exhortation, he continued to scratch himself all the time, and Polissena, when she heard his preachings and saw his scratch-

ings, planned a joke which she determined to play off on him, hoping thereby
to put a stop to his complaints about
her conduct, and it happened that this
jest of hers came to exactly the issue she
had forecast.   Turning to her son with
a mischievous smile she said : 'Panfilio,
you are always grieving and complaining
to me concerning the evil life which —
as you affirm — I lead.   I own that my
life is not a seemly one, and that your
warnings and counsels thereanent mark
you to be a good son ; but I ask you
now whether you will do one single
thing to please me, to serve as a proof
that you are indeed as jealous of my
honour as you protest.   If you will consent to this, I, for my part, promise to
place myself in your hands, and to have
done with all my lovers, and to lead a
good and holy life ; but if you fail to
gratify me in this respect, be sure that
I will pay no regard to your wishes, but
will give myself over to a course yet
more vicious than any I have hitherto

followed.' The son, who longed to see his mother return to an honest way of life more than for anything else in the world, made answer to her thus : ' Command me to do what you will, my mother; for even were you to bid me throw myself into the fire and be there consumed to ashes, I would willingly carry out your wishes, if thereby I might be able to free you from the shame and infamy of the life you now lead.' ' Listen then well to what I am going to say to you,' said Polissena, ' and consider my words, for if you shall diligently carry out the injunctions I lay upon you, everything you wish shall be fully granted to you; but if, on the other hand, you should fail in your promise, you will find yourself in a deeper state of ignominy than ever before.' ' I bind myself to observe and perform any duty or task you may put upon me,' said Panfilio. 'Then,' replied his mother, 'I will tell you what thing this is I require you to do. It is nothing more

arduous, my son, than that you should
promise you will not scratch your scabs
for three whole evenings. If you will
observe this light request of mine, I
will, on my part, satisfy your wishes.'

Panfilio, when he listened to the
proposition made by his mother, sat for
some time in thinking thereanent, and
though, itching as he did, he knew full
well that this condition of hers would
prove no easy one to observe, he nevertheless accepted it with joy, and as a
token of good faith shook hands with
his mother upon the bargain. When
the first of the evenings appointed for
the trial had come, Panfilio, having left
his workshop, went home, and throwing
off his cloak began to walk up and down
the room. After a little, finding himself somewhat cold, he sat down in a
corner of the chimney close to the fire,
and then the troublesome itch, provoked
by the heat, began to molest him so
sharply that he was sorely distressed and
longed to scratch himself to get some

ease. The mother, who was a very cunning jade, had taken good care to have a hot fierce fire on the hearth, in order that Panfilio might be well heated, and now, when she saw him writhing and stretching himself out after the manner of a snake, she said to him, ' Panfilio, what is it you do? Take good heed that you break not your promise, for if you keep your word I will assuredly keep mine.' To this Panfilio made answer: ' Have no doubt of my constancy, mother. See that you are firm yourself, for I will keep my pledge.' And all the while they were thus talking they were both of them raging with desire, the one to scratch his itching hide, and the other to find herself once more with one or other of her lovers.

Thus the first evening passed, bringing great discomfort both to mother and son, and when the second came, Polissena again caused to be made a large fire, and having got ready a good supper awaited her son's return. Panfilio, firm-

ly set on keeping his word, clenched his
teeth and put up with his trouble as well
as he could, and thus the second evening went by without any misadventure.
Polissena, when she saw how steadfast
in his determination Panfilio was, and
considered how two evenings had already
gone by without his having scratched
himself at all, began to fear greatly that
after all she would be the loser, and,
mightily disturbed in spirit, began to
lament her luckless case.   For all this
time she was strongly assailed by the
pricks of amorous desire, and spent her
time in devising some · scheme whereby
Panfilio might be driven once more to
scratch his skin, and she herself in consequence of his failure to keep his promise,
be free to wanton with her paramours.
So for the next evening she made ready
a delicate supper, with no lack of costly
and heady wine, and awaited the coming
of her son.   When Panfilio returned
and remarked the unwonted luxury of
their evening meal, he was greatly as-

tonished thereat, and, turning to his
mother, he said: 'Mother, for what
reason have you set out such a princely
feast as this? Is it possible that you
have indeed changed your mind?' To
this Polissena made answer: 'Certainly
not, my son; I am more firmly set in
my purpose than ever, but by chance
the thought struck me how you work
hard every day at your trade, from early
morn till nightfall, and besides this I
could not fail to notice how sorely this
accursed itch has worn and emaciated
your body, scarcely leaving any life in
you; so I felt deep compassion for your
suffering, and was moved to set before
you some more delicate dish than is our
wont to eat, in order that you might
gather strength therefrom, and assist
nature to withstand more readily the
torments which you have to endure
from the itch.

Panfilio, who was young and simple,
did not detect his mother's cunning
scheme, nor espy the snake that was

hidden amongst these fair flowers of her
kindness, but at once set himself down
to the table close to the fire, and began
with his mother to eat with zest and to
drink his wine with a merry heart.   But
the cunning and malicious Polissena
would now go and poke up the logs
and blow the fire in order to make it
burn all the fiercer, and now ply the poor
fellow with the delicate savoury dishes,
which were highly seasoned with all manner of spices, so that his blood might be
more and more inflamed by the food
and the warmth of the fire, and he himself be forced, on this account, to scratch
his itch.   Therefore, at last, when Panfilio had sat for some time close to the
fire and filled his belly to repletion, such
a fury of itching came over him that he
felt he must die if he could not scratch
himself; but, by dint of twisting his
body and fidgetting now to this side and
now to that, he endured the torment as
best he could.

But after a while the heat of the food,

which had been carefully salted and seasoned with this intent, and the Greek
wine, and the scorching fire, inflamed
his blood so direly that the wretched
Panfilio found his torment greater than
he could bear; so, tearing open his shirt
and laying bare his chest, and untrussing
his hose, and turning up his sleeves over
his elbows, he set to scratching himself
with such a will that the blood began to
run down from all parts of him as if it
had been sweat, and, turning to his
mother, who was laughing heartily to
herself, he cried in a loud voice: ' Let
each one enjoy his own fancy! Let each
one enjoy his own fancy! ' The mother,
although she saw clearly that the game
was now hers, feigned to be grieved
amain, and said to Panfilio, ' My son,
what folly is this of yours? What is it
that you would do? Is this the way
you keep the promise you have made
me? Of a truth you will never again
be able to throw it in my teeth that I
have not kept faith with you.' Panfilio

listened, scratching himself with all his might the while, and answered his mother with a troubled mind : ' Mother, let us for the future follow the bent which best pleases us. You must go about your business, and I will go about mine.' And from this hour the son never dared to question his mother as to her course of life, and she went back to her old habits, entertaining her lovers in freer measure even than before.

All the listeners were mightily pleased with this fable told by Cateruzza, and after they had spent some time in merry discourse thereanent, the Signor called upon the damsel to propound her enigma, and she, not wishing to interrupt the accustomed order of the entertainment, smilingly gave it in these words :

> What thing is that we ladies prize:
> Five fingers' breadth will tell its size;
> Divers fair nooks you find inside;
> No outlet, though the gate is wide;
> The first attempt will give us pain,
> For free access is hard to gain;

But later will grow long and straight,
And large and small accommodate ?

Cateruzza's obscurely worded enigma
gave abundant matter to the ladies and
gentlemen to consider; but, carefully as
they debated it from every point, and
turned it over and over again in their
minds, they were not able to hit upon
its real interpretation. Wherefore the
prudent Cateruzza, seeing that they
were all still wandering in obscurity and
unable to grasp the meaning of her riddle, said promptly, "So as not to keep
this honourable company any longer in
suspense, I will give forthwith the interpretation of my enigma, subjecting
myself, however, in this to the judgment
of others, who may be much wiser than
myself. My enigma, dear ladies, signifies nothing else than the glove which
you wear to protect your hand; this,
you know, will sometimes cause you
slight hurt when you first put it on, but
soon accommodates itself to your pleasure."

This explanation was held to be quite satisfactory by the honourable company, and when Cateruzza had ceased speaking the Signora gave a sign to Lauretta, who sat at Vicenza's side, to take her turn at the story-telling. And she, with a pretty boldness of mien and speech, turned her bright face towards Bembo, and said: "Signor Antonio, it were a great shame if you, kindly and gallant gentleman as you are, did not tell the company some fable with your wonted grace and talent. I, for my part, would willingly relate one, but just now I cannot call to mind one which would be at the same time pleasing and droll. Therefore, I beg you, Signor Antonio, that you will bear the burden in my place, and if you grant me this favour, I shall ever consider I am greatly beholden to you." Bembo, who had in no way prepared himself for story-telling this evening, answered: "Signora Lauretta, although I feel myself very unfit for the task, yet—seeing

that a request from you is as potent
with me as a command — I will accept
the charge you lay upon me, and will
strive to satisfy your wishes, at least in
part." And the Signora having given
her gracious permission, he began his
story in these words.

THE FOURTH FABLE.

*A dispute having arisen between three sisters of
a convent as to which of them should fill the
post of abbess, the bishop's vicar decides that
the office shall fall to the one who shall give
the most eminent proof of her worthiness.*

OWEVER great may be the
charm which modesty lends
to people in general, I, nevertheless, rate it far higher, dear
ladies, when one meets it in a man who
knows his own self. Wherefore, with
the good leave of the gracious ladies
around me, I purpose to tell a story no
less cleverly put together than pleasant,
which, though it may prove somewhat

overcharged with ridicule and wanting
in decency, I will do my best to relate
to you in modest and seemly terms,
such as are due and proper. And if
perchance at any time my narrative
should affront your chaste ears, I would
now forestall your pardon for the offence, entreating you to hold back your
censure till some future season.

In the noble city of Florence there is
a certain convent with an illustrious
reputation for holiness of life and for
religion; the name of it I will not give
just now, for fear of marring its fair
fame by any spot of scandal. It happened that the abbess of this house, who
was afflicted by many and heavy in-
firmities, came to the end of her days,
and rendered up her soul to her Creator.
Wherefore, she being dead and her body
buried with all the solemn rites of the
Church, the surviving sisters caused a
meeting of the chapter to be summoned
by the ringing of the bell, so that all
those who had a voice therein might

be called together. The vicar of mon-
signor the bishop, a prudent man and a
learned, and one moreover who desired
that the election of the new abbess
should be carried out according to the
strict letter of the law, gave the word to
the assembled sisters to be seated and
spake thus to them : 'Most respected
ladies, you know well enough, I con-
clude, that the sole reason why you are
gathered together here to-day is in order
that you may make choice of some one
who shall be the head over you. If this
be so, at the bidding of the conscience
which is in each of you it behoves you
to elect the one who appears to you all
the best fitted for the office.' And all
the sisters made answer that this was the
course they were minded to follow.

Now it happened that in the convent
there were three nuns betwixt whom
there sprang up a very keen contention
as to which of the three should be the
new abbess, because each one had a certain following amongst the sisters, and

had the reputation of being held in honour by other superiors, wherefore all
three of these greatly desired the title of
abbess.   While the sisters were getting
ready for the election of their new head,
one of the three nuns just mentioned,
named Sister Veneranda, rose from her
seat, and turning towards the other sisters, addressed them : ' My sisters, and
my children, whom I hold in such high
affection, you can understand well enough
with what loving zeal I have ever given
my best energies for the service of the
convent, so that I have not only grown
old therein, but am become veritably
decrepit.   Therefore, on account of my
long service and of my advanced age, it
seems to me only just and proper that I
should be elected as your head, and if
my long-continued labours and the vigils
and prayers of my youth fail to persuade
you to choose me, at least let my infirm
old age appeal to your consideration;
for to this, above every other thing, your
reverence is due.   It must be apparent

'to you that I can reckon on only a very short span of further life. Wherefore you may be sure that I shall, before long, make way for some other of you. For this reason, my well-beloved daughters, I beg that you will give me this brief season of ease and pleasure, and keep well in your hearts all the good counsels which I have ever given you.' And Veneranda, having finished her speech, weeping the while, was silent.

The appeal of the first sister being finished, Sister Modestia, a woman of middle age, rose from her seat and spake in this wise: 'Mothers and sisters mine, you have heard without concealment, and you must have clearly understood the claims put forward by Sister Veneranda, who happens to be the most advanced in age of any of us; but this fact, in my estimation, gives her no special claim to be chosen as our abbess, inasmuch as she is now come to such a time of life that, through senility, she has too much of simplicity and too little of counsel, and before long will herself require to be controlled and cared for, in lieu of controlling us. But if you, in your mature judgment, give due consideration to my good estate, and to the trust that is due to me, and remember of what ancestry I come, you cannot, of a surety, for the debt each of you owes to conscience, choose any other one but me to be your abbess. Our convent—as every one of you must know—is greatly vexed with processes and suits at law and has much need of support and protection, and what greater defence could you furnish to the monastery against its adversaries than the countenance and patronage of my family, who would give—supposing that I am elected your head—not merely their wealth and goods in your defence, but even their lives.'

Scarcely had Sister Modestia resumed her seat when Sister Pacifica rose to her feet, and, with the guise of deep humility, spake as follows: ' I am well assured, most honoured sisters, nay, I may take

it for certain that you, prudent and well-
advised ladies as you all are, will feel no
little astonishment that I, who came as
it were yesterday to abide amongst you,
should desire to put myself on an equali-
ty with, or even to supersede the two
most honoured sisters who have already
spoken. These ladies, both on the score
of age and of experience, are far above
me ; but if, with the eyes of the under-
standing, you come to consider carefully
how many and how great are my qualifications, of a surety you will rate more
highly my fresh youth than the decrepit
age of the one and the family claims of
the other. I — as all of you must know
quite well — brought with me hither a
very rich dowry, by the aid of which your
convent, which had fallen wellnigh to
ruin through the lapse of time, has been
reconstructed from roof to foundation.
I say nought about the houses and the
farms which have been bought with the
money of my dowry, from which every
year the house gains a great sum in the

shape of rent.   Wherefore, on account
of these and of other qualifications of
mine, and as a recompense for the many
and great benefits you have received
from me, it is your duty to choose me
as your abbess, seeing that your food
and your raiment depend (under God)
upon my bounty,' and having thus
spoken she sat down.

When the three sisters had thus
brought their discourses to a conclusion,
the vicar of the lord bishop summoned
all the nuns into his presence one after
another, and bade them write down the
name of the sister whom, upon their
conscience, they wished to be raised to
the dignity of abbess.   When this had
been done, and when all the sisters had
recorded their votes, it was found that
all the three were equal as to the number of votes given for each, nor was
there any difference between them.   On
this account there 'arose amongst all the
sisters a very acrimonious dispute, and
some wished to have the first named,

and some the second, and some the third,
for their head ; nor could there be found
any way of pacifying the contention.
Whereupon the bishop's vicar, perceiving how dogged was the obstinacy of
each faction, and bearing in mind that
each one of the three sisters might well
be promoted to the honourable office of
abbess for the special qualifications duly
cited, cast about in his mind to devise a
a way and means whereby one of the
three might retain the post of abbess
without giving any cause of offence or
disaffection to the others. He ordered
the three sisters who-sought the office
to be summoned into his presence, and
thus addressed them : ' Well-beloved
sisters, I comprehend fully your many
virtues and your many qualifications,
and I cannot but say that either one of
you would be in the highest sense worthy
to be chosen as abbess of thi convent.
But between you three honourable sisters the contest for election has been
amazingly severe, and the votes given

for each of you have proved to be equal in number. On this account—in order that you may continue your peaceful lives in love and quietness—I hereby propose to you to employ in the election of your abbess a method which—as I hope—shall lead to the contention being brought to an end to the satisfaction of you all. The method which I suggest is this: each one of you three sisters, who have put forth your claims to succeed to the office of abbess, shall exercise herself for the next three days to perform in our presence some special feat which shall be praiseworthy in itself and worthy of being held in remembrance, and whichever of these three sisters shall show herself able to perform the feat the most capable and most worthy of future fame shall be, by the good consent of all the sisters, duly chosen abbess, and to her shall be accorded all the honour and reverence which of right belong to her.'

This proposition of the bishop's vicar

won the approbation of the three sisters,
on which account they all with one voice
promised to observe the conditions laid
down. And when the day appointed for
the trial had come, and all the nuns belonging to the convent were gathered
together in the chapter house, the vicar
caused to be brought before him the
three sisters who aspired to mount up
to the high post of abbess, and questioned them severally as to whether they
had given due thought to their affairs
in the matter of performing some noteworthy feat as he had ordained, and they
all gave answer that they had. Après[1]
estans toutes assises Sœur Venerande,
qui estoit la plus aagée de toutes, se mit
au milieu de la place, et tirant de sa cu-
cule une petite eguille de damas, laquelle
y estoit attachée, leva ses robbes et sa
chemise par devant, puis haulsant une
cuisse en la presence de tous les assis-
tans, pissa si delicattement au travers du
trou de l'eguille, qu'une seule petite

[1] Translation by Pierre de la Rivey.

goutte ne tomba a terre que premier elle n'eust passe par le trou. Quoy voyant, le grand vicaire et les religieuses, pensèrent indubitablement que Venerande deust estre abbesse, jugeans estre impossible pouvoir faire chose plus subtille que ceste là. Ce faict, Sœur Modestie, que n'estoit de beaucoup si vielle que l'autre, se leva, et s'estant mise en place marchande, tira de son sein un dé dont on joue, et le mit sur un banc, les cinq points dessus. Après print cinq petits grains de millet et mit chacun d'iceux en l'un des cinq points du dé ; puis descouvrant son derriere et approchant ses fesses du banc sur lequel estoit le dé, fit un pet si gros et terrible, qu'il fit quasi évanouir de peur le grand vicaire et toutes les religieuses, et encore que ce pet sortist avec un bruict violent et sifflement horrible, si fut il neantmoins tiré d'une belle addresse et dexterité, que le grain qui estoit au trou du milieu demeura en sa place, et les autres disparurent et ne furent jamais veus depuis. Toute l'as-

Sister Pacifique Proves Her
Worthiness

Flight the Sixth

FOURTH FABLE

Sister Pacifique Proves Her Worthiness

Night the Sixth
FOURTH FABLE

Sister Pacifique Proves Her Worthiness

Night the Sixth

FOURTH FABLE

ter *Pacifique* Proves Her

Sister Pacifique **Proves Her** Worthiness

Night the Sixth

FOURTH FABLE

semblée ne trouva ceste espreuve moin-
dre que l'autre ; cependant demeuroit
coye, attendant se que feroit Sœur Pacifique ; laquelle, se mettant en jeu comme
les autres, fit un tour, non d'une vieille,
mais d'une jeune hommasse, pour ce
qu'ayant tiré de sa pochette un noyau
de pesche le jecta en l'air, puis soudain
se retrousa par derriere, levant le cul en
haut, et recevant le noyau avec les fesses,
l'estreignit si fort qu'elle le grugea plus
menu que n'est menue la poussière.
The vicar, who was a man sage and
well-advised, began forthwith to confer
with the sisterhood and to give mature
consideration to the amazing feats per-
formed by the three competing sisters,
and when, after a time, he perceived that
there was little prospect of coming to a
decision, he took time to deliberate as
to what the final judgment should be.
And, forasmuch as he was not able to
find in his learned books aught which
might guide him in deciding this matter,
he let it go as a thing not to be solved,

and even to this our day the dispute is still pending. Wherefore I call upon you, most learned and prudent ladies, to disentangle this question, which, on account of its importance, I should not venture myself to approach.

This story of Bembo's proved to be more a source of mirth to the men than to the ladies, seeing that the latter for very shame hid their faces in their laps and did not dare to look up. But the men discussed now one incident and now another of the story they had just listened to, and gathered no little diversion therefrom, till at last the Signora, noticing that their laughter was somewhat unbecoming, and that the ladies sat as though they had been changed into so many marble statues, commanded silence and put an end to the unseemly laughter, in order that Bembo might follow the accustomed rule by giving his enigma. But he, who had already spoken as much as was meet, turned towards the fair Lauretta and

said : " It is now your turn, Signora
Lauretta, to set an enigma. I may indeed have satisfied you in one matter,
but that is no reason why I should satisfy you in another." And the lady,
who had no wish to make delay by her
refusal, thus began in order to relieve
herself of her obligation :

> A riddle I would have you guess ;
> And though its meaning savours less
> Of ruse than of a ribald jest,
> I'll beg you take it at its best.
> First I to my companion go,
> He up above, and I below ;
> Then something hard I take in hand,
> And temper it with unguent bland,
> And place it where it ought to go ;
> Then work it featly to and fro,
> And swing and sway it up and down,
> Until success my efforts crown.

Everyone declared that the enigma
proposed by Lauretta was fully as in-
teresting as the story of Bembo, and,
because it seemed as if few or any of
the company could fathom its meaning,

the Signora directed her to give the interpretation thereof. Then Lauretta, so as not to interpose any further delay, spake thus: " My riddle means that there were two men who set to work to saw in pieces a huge beam of wood. One of these took in his hand the saw, which is a very hard thing, and went up above, while the other remained in the saw-pit beneath. The first then smeared the saw with oil, and placed it in the fissure of the beam, and then the two companions working together handled the saw up and down in order to accomplish their task."

The ingenious interpretation of this enigma gave the greatest pleasure to all the company, and, after the talk had ceased, the Signora gave command to Eritrea to begin the telling of her fable, and she straightway spake as follows.

THE FIFTH FABLE.

Pre Zefiro works a spell on a youth whom he finds eating figs in his garden.

IT has often been said, dearest ladies, that there are mysterious virtues abiding in words, and in herbs, and in stones; but stones assuredly may be held to excel both herbs and words in persuasive powers, as you will clearly see by this little tale of mine.

There once lived in the city of Bergamo a miserly priest, called Pre Zefiro, who by common report was said to be possessed of great wealth. This man had a garden situated beyond the city walls, near the gate which is called Penta. This same garden was surrounded in such a manner by walls and ditches that neither man nor beast could enter therein, and it was well planted with fruit-trees of every kind, and amongst others

there was a great fig-tree with branches
spreading on all sides, and laden every
season with beautiful and excellent fruit,
of which the priest was wont to partake
every year with all the gentlemen and
notables of the city. These figs were
of a mixed colour, between white and
purple, and they dropped tears of juice
which were like honey. So precious
were they, that they were always carefully guarded by watchmen. One night,
when by chance the guardians were not
on the watch, a youth clambered up
into this fig-tree, and, having chosen the
ripest figs, silently set to work to stow
them away in their skins, just as they
were, in the storehouse of his belly.

Pre Zefiro, having suddenly remem-
bered that there were no watchmen in
his garden, flew thither, and straightway
saw the fellow sitting in the tree and
eating figs at his leisure. Whereupon
the priest began to beg him to come
down, but as he took no heed of his
words, Pre Zefiro threw himself on his

knees and conjured him by heaven, by
the earth, by the planets, by the stars,
by the elements, and by all the sacred
words which are written in the Scriptures,
to come down from the tree; but still
the youth ate steadily on. Pre Zefiro,
seeing that he gained no advantage whatever by these adjurations, gathered certain herbs which grew round about in
the garden, and once more conjured the
fellow by the virtue which dwelt therein
to come down, but he only clambered
up higher so that he might fill himself
with greater ease. Then the priest
spake as follows: 'It is written that in
words, and in herbs, and in stones, there
are hidden virtues. I have conjured you
by the first two, and they have availed
nothing to bring you down out of the
tree, now by virtue of the third I once
more conjure you to come down to the
ground.' So straightway he began to
hurl stones at the thief with great ran-
cour and fury, smiting him now on the
arm, now on the leg, now on the spine;

so that at last the youth, swollen and
bethumped and bruised as he was on
account of the frequent blows he had
received, was obliged to come down from
his perch. Then he took to flight, having first given back to Pre Zefiro all
the figs which he had stowed away in
his bosom. And thus stones proved
themselves to be more potent as instruments of exorcism than either words
or herbs.

Eritrea had no sooner come to the
end of her brief story than the Signora
bade her to follow it up with her enigma,
so without further delay she spake as
follows :

> Gallant knights and ladies gay,
> Tell me truthfully, I pray ;
> Answer quick to my behest,
> Which of three you like the best ?
> That which is bound close and tight,
> Or that makes you writhe by night,
> Or that which in the evening grey
> Will drive you from your bed away.
> If my speech you fathom well,
> Tell me, gentles, quickly tell.

All the listeners were mightily perplexed over this cunningly-devised enigma propounded by Eritrea, and no one
knew what answer to give. But the Signora pressed each one to give an opinion,
and one gave preference to the narrow
and well tied, another to the turn which
comes early, and another that of the first
watches of the night. Nevertheless not
one of them understood the true signification of the riddle. Wherefore Eritrea,
when she saw their want of agreement,
said : ' It does not seem right that my
gracious hearers should remain any longer in doubt, so I will say at once that the
thing which is bound close and tight is
the scurf on the skin, which, if one wants
to be cured of it, must be doctored and
tied up tightly with bandages. The
thing which causes a man to leave his
bed in the night is the flux, since one
suffering therewith must needs find relief. The last named, which touches one
in the evening hour, is the troublesome
itch, which, when night is coming on,

heats the blood, and causes such intolerable irritation that one with it upon him is fain to tear his flesh with his teeth, as did the widow's son in the learned and elegant story we have lately heard from Cateruzza.'

The ingenious explanation set forth by Eritrea to her very knotty riddle gave universal satisfaction, and when the listeners had all taken leave of the Signora, the hour being now late, they went their several ways, under promise to return the next evening to their wonted place of meeting.

The End of the Sixth Night.

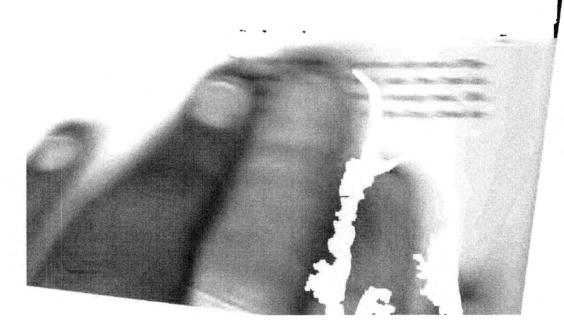

List of Illustrations.

VOLUME TWO.

Here endeth the Second Volume.

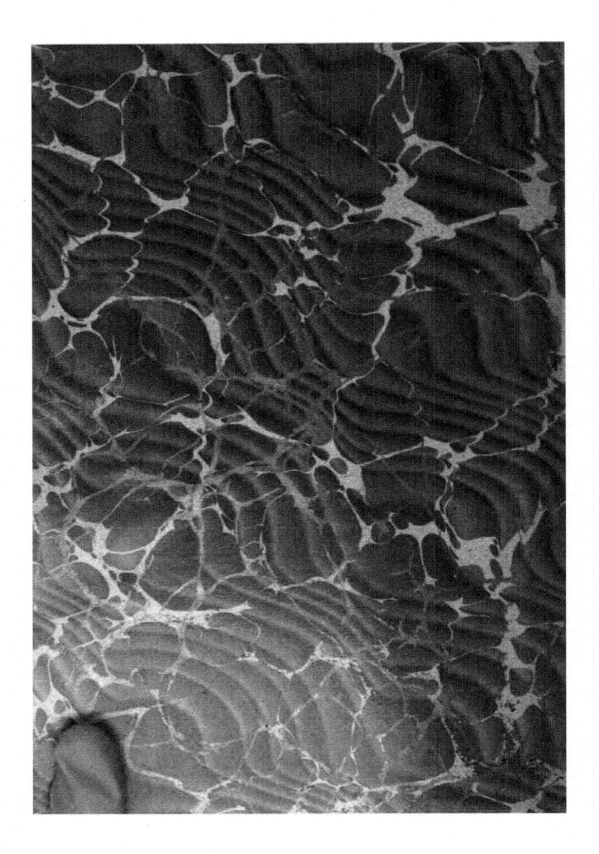